RUNNING WILD

ILLUSTRATED BY SARAH YOUNG

HarperCollins *Children's Books*

First published in hardback in Great Britain by HarperCollins *Children's Books* 2009
First published in paperback in Great Britain by HarperCollins *Children's Books* 2010

HarperCollins *Children's Books* is a division of HarperCollins*Publishers* Ltd
77-85 Fulham Palace Road, Hammersmith, London W6 8JB

This edition produced 2011 for
The Book People, Hall Wood Avenue, Haydock, St Helens, WA11 9UL

2

Visit us on the web at www.harpercollins.co.uk

Text copyright © Michael Morpurgo 2009
Illustrations © Sarah Young 2009

ISBN 978-0-00-790965-0

Michael Morpurgo and Sarah Young reserve the right to be identified
as the author and illustrator of the work.

Printed and bound in England by Clays Ltd, St Ives plc

A sudden change of heart

he sea murmured onto the beach.
Beneath me, the elephant walked
on over soft and silent sand. The
further we went along the beach
away from the hotel, away from the
distant cries of the swimmers in the sea, the quieter
everything became. I was loving the gentle rock and roll
of the ride. I closed my eyes and breathed in the
peace around me. This was a million miles from

everything that had happened, from everything that had brought me here.

It was as I was riding up there on the elephant, swaying in the sun, that Dad's elephant joke came into my mind. Usually I can't remember jokes, but I always remembered this one, maybe because Dad told it so often. I knew it word for word, just as he'd tell it.

"You know the one about the elephant and the bananas, Will?" he'd begin, and without waiting for an answer, off he'd go. "A man and a boy were sitting opposite one another in this railway carriage – they were travelling between Salisbury and London. On his lap, the man had a huge paper bag full of bananas. But soon enough, the boy noticed that something very strange was going on here. The man wasn't eating the bananas. Instead, every few minutes, he'd just stand up, open the window, and throw one of them out. Of course, the boy couldn't understand what he was doing this for. He kept trying to puzzle it out. So in the end, he just had to ask.

"'Scuse me,' he says, "but could you tell me why you're throwing all those bananas out of the window?"

"To keep the elephants away," replies the man. "Cos elephants is very dangerous, y'know."

millions of them out there, squillions. And elephants is very dangerous, y'know."

I loved that joke, mostly because when Dad was telling it, he'd always be heaving with laughter before he could ever finish it, and I loved to hear Dad's laugh. Whenever he was home it was his laugh that filled the house, brought it alive again.

I didn't want to think about that, because I knew where it would lead, and I didn't want to go there. So I tried to make myself think of a train journey instead, a train journey when Dad hadn't been there. I wanted to keep Dad out of the picture. I didn't want to have to remember, not now, not again. But memories of the train journey with Mum came tumbling out, out of my control and out of sequence, as memories often are, because memories will always become other memories, I suppose – they cannot help themselves.

I always wanted train journeys to go on for ever, and especially this one. I liked trains, the rattle and the rhythm of them. I loved to press my forehead against the cold of the glass, and trace a single raindrop with my finger as it found its way down across the window. I'd be gazing out at the countryside rushing by, at cows and horses scattering away over the fields, at clouds of starlings whirling in the wind, at a formation of geese flying high into the evening sun.

And I'd be on the lookout for wild animals, for foxes or rabbits, or even a deer. A glimpse of just one of these

long as you're passing through, just so long as you leave us alone. I had always longed to be part of their world. For me that momentary glimpse was never enough, always too quickly over.

On this train journey though I had seen no foxes, no deer, not even a rabbit, and that was because I hadn't been looking for them. My mind was elsewhere. I didn't want it to be, but it was. Everything out there was nothing but a blur of grey skies and green fields, interrupted with monotonous regularity by endless passing telegraph poles. None of it was of any interest to me. I wanted this train journey to go on forever, not because I was enjoying it one bit, but simply because I did not want to go where I was going. I did not want to arrive.

I glanced up at Mum sitting beside me, but she did not look back at me. I could see she was lost deep in her thoughts, and I knew well enough what they had to be, that they were much the same as mine, and that it was better not to interrupt them. I regretted again that I'd yelled at her at breakfast that morning. I shouldn't have done it, but it had been the shock of it, the suddenness. She'd just said it, right out of the blue, without any warning at all. "We're going back home, Will, as soon as I've packed the cases. Grandma says she'll drive us to the station."

I tried arguing, but she wouldn't listen. So that was when I yelled at her, and did a runner to the hay-barn, climbing up the stack to the very top. I sat sulking there, till Grandpa came and found me, and fetched me down. Mum was very upset, he told me, and we shouldn't be upsetting her, not after everything that had happened. He was right of course. I hadn't meant to do it, but I'd been so looking forward to staying for Christmas down on the farm with Grandpa and Grandma. It was the house where Dad had grown up, the place we'd always been for every single Christmas of my life, whether Dad was home on leave or not.

But if I'm honest, that wasn't the only reason I'd

_____ she'd come out with it at breakfast that morning she'd never even discussed it. She'd just told me. It wasn't like her. Mum always talked things over with me, always.

After all, hadn't she been the one, who only a few weeks before had insisted that it was a good idea to go to stay with Grandpa and Grandma, to get away from home, and the memories, and the ghosts? Hadn't Mum explained to me that she thought we should be with Grandpa and Grandma at this time anyway, because after all, weren't we all going through the same thing, and wouldn't it be good for us to do it together? So why this sudden change of heart?

I gazed blankly out of the train window, trying to work it all out. I thought then it might have been because she had just had enough of Grandma. And it was true that Grandma was never the easiest person in the world to get on with. She did like to organise, to try and tell everyone what to do, what not to do, and what to think even. With Grandma everything had to be just so, and that could be a bit irksome at times, and annoying. But as Mum was forever telling me, that was just how Grandma was and we had to put up with it, like Grandpa did.

No, we couldn't be leaving because of Grandma. It didn't make any sense. But if it wasn't Grandma, what was it then? It certainly wasn't Grandpa, and it certainly wasn't the farm. For Mum and for me, for all of us, it had always been just about the best place in the whole world, and my idea of heaven. I loved being there, whatever the weather. I was up before breakfast with Grandpa, milking the cows, and feeding the calves, and then opening up the hens and geese on the way back to the house for breakfast. Afterwards, it was out on the tractor, with Grandpa again – and driving it sometimes too, when we were far enough away from the farmhouse for Grandma not to be able to spot us. We'd be checking the sheep together, counting the lambs, or mending fences when we had to. We'd be doing whatever it was

...talking about it too. Grandma said one afternoon when Grandpa and I came in for our tea: "Happy as Larry out on the farm, aren't you, Will? Give you half a chance, and I reckon you'd be sleeping in your wellies. You're just like your Grandpa."

She was right about that. For a start Grandpa never said a lot, and nor did I. We knew each other so well that maybe we just didn't need to. Grandpa never mentioned anything about what had happened, except once, when we were down in the milking parlour together, washing down after milking. "Got something to say to you, Will," he began. "What I think is this, and I've thought a lot about it. In fact these last weeks, I've thought about precious little else. When you've cut yourself, what you do is you make sure the wound is clean, and you put a plaster on it, don't you? Then you give it time to heal – if you understand what I'm saying. You don't keep taking the plaster off and looking at it, because if you do, you'll just be reminded of how much it hurts. And you don't keep asking yourself why it had to happen to you in the first place either, because that won't make it better. Sometimes – and I know it's not what some people think these days – but sometimes when you're hurting, I think the less said the better. So you and me, Will, we'll say no more about it, unless you want to, that is."

But I didn't want to, and so between us, nothing was ever said about it again. And in fact, Grandma hardly spoke of it either, not in front of me anyway. It became like an unspoken pact between all of us, to say nothing, and I was glad of it. I knew well enough that they were doing it for me, to spare me the pain. They were trying their very best to take my mind off it.

But the trouble was that it was always there, in the back of our minds, despite all that Grandma and Grandpa were doing to keep everyone busy and happy. And we *were* happy, as happy as it was possible to be, under the circumstances anyway. But as each evening came to an end, and the time came for me to go upstairs

come flooding back, the ache inside me, the pity of it, and worst of all, the awful finality of it. I longed every night for sleep to come, so that I wouldn't have to remember it all again, so that my mind wouldn't go over it and churn it all up. But the more I longed for sleep it seemed, the more it was denied me. I'd lie there listening to the murmur of their talk downstairs in the kitchen.

If I tried, I could hear most of what they were saying. I didn't want to eavesdrop, but sometimes I couldn't stop myself. I'd hear Mum sobbing again, and Grandma sometimes as well. Soon enough I would find myself crying too, and once I'd started I knew I wouldn't be able to stop, not until I fell asleep, because everything Mum was saying down there in the kitchen seemed to echo so closely everything I was feeling.

It was her words I was hearing again in my head now, as I rode along the beach on the elephant. Ahead of us a large lizard or iguana skittered away over the sand and disappeared into the shadows of the palm trees. A sea eagle soared out over the sea. There was so much to see, but my memory would not leave me in peace. I was doing all I could to force myself to live for now, to bask in the joy of the moment, in the beauty of this strange paradise, and for a while I could and I did, but not for long. So I determined that if I was going to have to relive anything in my mind, I would will it to be only the good times: driving the tractor with Grandpa, pulling off a newborn lamb and rubbing the warmth of life into her, seeing the fox padding across High Meadow early one morning.

But instead, all that came to my mind was everything I had overheard Mum saying down in the kitchen only a few nights before. Her words still fell just as heavily on my heart, as when I'd first heard them.

"Why did he have to go and leave us? What am I

supposed to tell Will, Grandma? I mean, how can you tell a nine-year-old? How can you explain the stupidity

...angry with him that sometimes I find myself almost hating him. Isn't that terrible? Isn't it? Back home, I have to pretend to everyone all the time, that it was all in a good cause, that I'm proud of him, and I'm brave, that I'm coping. Well I am proud of him, but I'm not coping, and I'm not brave, and it wasn't a good cause. Tell me why. Will someone tell me why? Why did he have to go? Why did it have to be him?"

When they came up to bed later, and Mum came in to kiss me goodnight as usual, I pretended to be asleep. I was crying silent tears, and when she'd gone out again, they kept on coming. All night long they kept coming. That night, I felt I would drown in sadness.

I knew that if I went on remembering like this I would only be making myself live through the same pain all over again. I wrenched my mind away from where it was taking me. From now on I would recall only the marvellous times, the magical moments that I knew would lift my spirits, that would banish all grieving, that would make me smile. I thought it was working too. I could almost feel Mum's arm come round me and hold me, and the coolness of her hand as she smoothed my hair above my ear. But then I remembered her doing it just like that back at home, on the last day the three of us had been together.

I could see it all in my head now, just as it had happened: Dad going off down the path in his uniform, Mum there beside me, watching him go, her arm round my shoulder, her hand smoothing my hair. After we'd waved him off, we stood there on the doorstep in our dressing gowns, watching the milk float come humming down the road.

"Don't worry, Will," she'd told me. "Dad's been out there twice before. He'll be fine. He'll be back home before you can say Jack Robinson, you'll see."

"Jack Robinson," I'd said. When I looked up at her moments later, I saw I'd made her smile through h~~

~~ it had all happened. A rainy Sunday it had been. We were flopped on the sofa in front of the television, watching *Shrek 2*, for about the tenth time. It was my favourite film – Dad had given me the DVD for my birthday a couple of months before. We were enjoying it just as much as ever, anticipating every wacky moment, every hilarious gag. The doorbell rang.

"Oh, for goodness' sake, who's that?" Mum said. She pressed the pause button, got up wearily from the sofa, and went to see who it was. I wasn't a bit interested in who it was, I just wanted to go on watching Shrek. There were hushed voices in the hallway. I heard footsteps going along the passage into the kitchen. The door closed. Whoever the visitors were, Mum obviously wasn't coming back into the sitting-room for a while. So

I pressed the play button and settled down again to watch. Only when the film finished, an hour or so later, did it occur to me that it was a little strange that Mum still hadn't come back – I knew she loved Shrek almost as much as I did. That's why I went to find her.

She was sitting alone at the kitchen table, her head lowered, her hands cupped round a mug of tea. She didn't look up when I came in, and she didn't speak for a while either. I could see then that something must be wrong. "Who was it?" I asked her. "At the door. Who was it?"

"Come and sit down, Will," she said, her voice so soft and far away that I could hardly hear her. When she looked up I could see that her eyes were red with crying. "It's your Daddy, Will. I told you where he went, didn't I? We found Iraq on the map, found where he was, didn't we? Well, there was a bomb by the side of the road, and he was in a Land Rover…" She reached out across the table and took my hands in hers. "He's dead, Will."

We sat there in silence for a few moments. I went to sit on her lap, because I knew that was what she

needed, what I needed too. We didn't cry. We just held
on to each other tight, as tight as we could. It felt to me

again all night long.

"Why, Mum? Why did he have to go to the war?"

It was a while before she replied. "Because he's a
soldier, Will," she told me. "When countries fight wars,
it's the soldiers who do the fighting. It's always been like
that. It's what soldiers have to do."

"I know that, Mum. Dad told me," I said. "But what
was the war for?"

She didn't answer me.

"Look at me, I need a smile"

he young *mahout* who was leading the elephant, sometimes by the ear, sometimes by the trunk, was wearing a long white shirt that flapped loosely about him. The elephant kept trying to curl his trunk round it, tugging at it. The *mahout* ignored him and walked on, speaking all the while to the elephant in confidential whispers. I longed to know what he was saying, but didn't dare ask.

He looked friendly enough, smiling at me whenever he glanced back up at me to see if I was all right. But he didn't seem to want to talk, and anyway I wasn't sure he spoke any English. But I knew that if we didn't get talking, then I'd be left alone again with my thoughts, and I didn't want that. And besides, I really wanted to find out more about this elephant I was riding. I decided to risk it and talk.

"What's he called?" I asked him.

"This elephant is not he. He is she," he told me, in near perfect English. "Oona. She is called Oona if you want to know. She is twelve years old, and she is like a sister to me. I know her from the first day she is born." Once the young man had started talking, he didn't seem to want to stop. He spoke very fast, too fast, and never once turned round, so he wasn't at all easy to understand. I had to listen hard.

He went on, trying all the while to extricate his shirt-tail from the grip of the elephant's trunk. "This elephant, she likes this shirt very much, and she also likes people. Oona is very friendly, very intelligent too, and naughty. She is very naughty sometimes, you would

not believe it. Sometimes she wants to run when I do not want her to run, and once she is running she is very hard to stop. Then once she is stopped, she is very difficult to start again. You know what Oona likes best? I tell you. She likes the sea. But it is a strange thing. Not today. Today she does not like the sea. I think maybe she is not feeling so good today. I take her down to the sea early this morning for her swim like I always do, and she does not want to go in. She does not want to go near. She only stands there looking out to sea as if she never saw it before. I tell her that the sea is the same as it was yesterday, but still she will not go in. One thing I know for sure: you can't make Oona do what Oona does not want to do."

He tugged his shirt free at last. "Thank you, Oona, very nice of you," he said, stroking her ear. "You see, she is happier now, and I think maybe this is because she likes you. I can tell this when I look in her eyes. It is how elephants speak, with their eyes. This is a true thing."

I did not ask any more questions after this, because I was far too busy just enjoying myself. I was savouring every moment of this ride. The elephant, I noticed then, was strangely mottled, with a sort of pink pigmentation under her grey skin. A pink elephant! I laughed out loud, and the elephant tossed her trunk as if she understood the joke and didn't much like it.

Everything I was seeing was new and exciting to me,

the deep blue of the waveless ocean on one side, the
shadowy green of the jungle on the other, where the

I was thinking that maybe Mum had been right, that this
was the perfect place to forget. But I didn't forget. I
couldn't.

Mum and I had drifted through the days like
sleepwalkers, enduring it all together, the phone calls,
the cards, the dozens of bunches of flowers left outside
our door. The television news kept showing the same
photograph of Dad, always in his uniform, never as he
was at home.

Then there was the silent drive to the airport with
Grandpa and Grandma in the front. Beside me in the
back seat, Mum looked steadfastly out of the window
all the way. But she did squeeze my hand from time
to time, to reassure me, and I would do the same in
return. It became a secret sign between us, a kind of

confidential code. One squeeze meant, 'I'm here. We'll get through this together'. Two meant, 'Look at me. I need a smile.'

Out on the tarmac of the windswept airfield, we stood and watched the plane land, and taxi to a standstill. A piper was playing, as the flag-covered coffin was borne out from inside the plane, slowly, slowly, by soldiers from Dad's regiment. After, there were more long days of silent sadness, with Grandma and Grandpa still staying on in the house and doing everything for us: Grandma cooking meals we didn't want to eat, Grandpa out in the garden trimming the hedges, mowing the lawn, weeding the flower bed, Grandma busying herself endlessly around the house, cleaning, tidying, polishing, ironing. There were telephone calls to answer, and the doorbell too. A lot of callers had to be kept at bay. Grandpa did that. There was the shopping to do as well. He did that too. Sometimes we did it together, and I liked that. It got me out of the house.

For the funeral, people lined the streets and the church was packed. A piper played a lament over the graveside in the rain, and soldiers fired a volley into the air. The echoes of it seemed to go on for ever. Afterwards

Well, I wouldn't, not so long as Mum was there beside me squeezing my hand, once, twice.

At the gathering of family and friends in the house afterwards, everyone seemed to be speaking in hushed voices over their teacups. I was longing for it to be over. I wanted them all to go. I wanted only to be left alone in the house with Mum. Grandpa and Grandma were the last to go. They'd been wonderful, I knew they had, but I could see Mum was as relieved as I was, when at last we said our goodbyes to them later that evening. We stood by our front gate and watched them drive away.

Two hand squeezes and a smile. It was over.

But it wasn't. Dad's fishing coat hung in the hallway, his Chelsea scarf round its shoulders. His boots were by the back door, still muddy from the last walk we'd all had together along the river to the pub. He'd bought me a packet of cheese and onion crisps that day, and there'd been a bit of an argument about that, because Mum had found the empty crisp packet in my anorak pocket afterwards – she always hated me eating that kind of food.

Whenever we went up to town to Stamford Bridge to see Chelsea play, Dad and I always had a pie and some crisps at the same pub, out in the street if it was fine weather, and everyone would be wearing blue. We'd walk to the ground afterwards. The whole street was a river of blue, and we were part of the river. I liked the ritual of getting to the match as much as the game itself. Sooner or later, after we got back home, Mum would always ask what we'd had for lunch, and we would always tell her, confess it sheepishly, and she would tell us both off. I loved it when we were both told off together – it was all part of it, of going to the football with Dad.

Dad's fishing rod was standing there in the corner by the deep freeze where it always was, and his ukulele lay where he'd left it on top of the piano. Beside it, there was the photo of Dad, smiling out at me, proudly holding up the ten-pound pike he'd caught. Often, when

       icon to me, a talisman. But now I tried all I could to avoid looking at it because I knew it would only make me feel sad again if I did. I felt bad about that, but I preferred to feel bad than sad. I was so filled up with sadness that there was no room for any more.

Some days I would wake up in the morning thinking and believing it had all been a nightmare, that Dad would be having his breakfast in the kitchen as usual when I got downstairs, that he'd be walking me to school as usual. Then I'd remember, and I'd know it was no nightmare, no dream, that the worst really had happened.

I was back at school a week or so after the funeral. Everyone was kind, too kind. I could tell that no one really wanted to talk to me. Even Charlie and Tonk and Bart, my best friends – they had been all my life – even they were keeping their distance. They didn't seem to know what to say to me. Nothing was how it had been. Everything and everyone was suddenly awkward. The teachers were all being sugary kind, Mr Mackenzie too, the head teacher – 'Big Mac', we all called him. He was sweetness itself, and that wasn't natural. No one was natural any more. Everyone was pretending. It made me feel alone, as if I didn't belong there any more.

One morning I decided I just couldn't stand it any more. I put my hand up in class, and asked if I could go to the toilet. But I didn't go to the toilet. I just walked out of the school, and went home. Mum wasn't there and the house was locked. I sat on the doorstep and waited for her. That's where Big Mac found me when he came looking for me. Even then he wasn't cross. Mum was called away from her work at the hospital. She was upset, I could see that, and told me how worried everyone had been, but she wasn't angry with me either. I was almost hoping she would be. It wasn't the only time I ran away.

One afternoon Mum met me at the school gates in
her nurse's uniform. I usually walked home on my own

'like a good boy'. That was when Mum told me.

"We've been thinking, Grandma and me, we've been
talking it over, Will," she began. "And we've decided
that you need more time to settle down, that maybe I
sent you back to school too soon, that maybe we've
rushed back into things too quickly – both of us, I mean.
People have been really kind, and really considerate.
Mr Mackenzie at school agreed at once, so did the
hospital. They all think we should go away for a while.
They've said that we can take as long as we like, and to
come back only when we're really ready to."

This all sounded more than fine to me, but when
Grandma interrupted, it got even better, because that
was when Grandma told me that she'd worked it all
out, that we would be coming down to stay on the farm

for a month or so. "I've told your mum, Will," she went on. "I said I won't take no for an answer. You'll be staying for Christmas, and for as long as you like afterwards, for as long as it takes." Mum and I exchanged a look and a smile at that, because Grandma never took no for an answer anyway.

"Grandma thinks it'll be a really good break for both of us, just what we need," Mum told me. "What do you think, Will?"

"All right," I said, with a shrug. But I was over the moon.

Every day of our stay had been brilliant, except that is for a surprise visit to the doctor for some sort of injection that Mum said was important. "All kids have it at your age," she explained. I protested, but I could see I was getting nowhere. In the doctor's surgery, I looked the other way as the needle went in, but it still hurt like hell. But that apart, and despite Grandma being her usual bossy self, I'd had the best of times.

So it had come as a complete surprise to me when Mum suddenly announced we wouldn't be staying on with Grandma and Grandpa for Christmas after all, but that the

suitcases were already packed and we'd be going home by
train that morning. Grandma was going to drive us to the

to me and told me to stay where I was, that she wouldn't
be long. She asked the driver if he'd mind waiting a
minute or two. She seemed suddenly excited, almost as
if she were trying to suppress a giggle.

"Where are you going, Mum?" I asked her, but she
was out of the taxi by now and running up the path into
the house. She didn't answer me. I couldn't make head
or tail of what was going on.

It wasn't long before she was out again carrying a
heavy suitcase. "Can you take us back to the station,
please?" she asked the driver.

"Take you to the moon, if you're paying, darling," he
said.

"Not going to the moon, not quite that far," Mum told
him breathlessly, as she climbed back into the taxi.

Then she told me to close my eyes. When I opened them again, she was flourishing two passports at me, a huge smile on her face. "Grandma's idea," she said, "and I promise you, Will, it's the best idea she ever had – actually I think it was Grandpa's. Anyway, she said that they thought it would be good for us to have Christmas away on our own, just the two of us, somewhere very special, somewhere we can forget... y'know, somewhere thousands of miles away."

She took a brochure out of her bag, and waved that at me too. "Look, Will! There's the hotel. There's the beach. There's the sea and the sand. And do you know where that is? Indonesia, where my family come from. I've never ever been there, and now I'm going, and you're coming with me. Full of surprises, your grandma. She never asked. Well, she wouldn't, would she? She just went ahead and booked it. 'A Christmas present from Grandpa and me,' she says. 'You just go and enjoy yourselves.'"

Mum's whole face was bright with laughter now. "All we needed were those injections – remember, Will? – then just our passports, our summer things, and we're on our way."

"What, now? We're going now?"

"Right now."

we a really laughed in a very long time. It turned to tears soon enough. Crying together, I discovered then, was so much better than crying alone. We clung to one another in the back of the taxi, and at last began to let go of our grief.

At the station, the taxi driver helped us out with the suitcases. He wouldn't accept any payment. "It's on me," he said, taking Mum by the hand, and helping her out. "It took me a while to work out who you were. I was in the crowd outside the church at the funeral. I saw you and the lad. I was a soldier once myself. In the Falklands. A while ago, but you don't forget. Lost my best friend out there. You have a good holiday now, I reckon you deserve it."

I'd been on a plane a few times before, to

Switzerland. But this plane was massive. It took an age lumbering down the runway before it lifted off. There was a moment when I thought it never would. I had my own screen, so that I could choose whatever film I wanted. I watched *Shrek 2*, again. When it finished, I happened to pick up Mum's holiday brochure. I opened it. The first picture I saw was of an orang-utan gazing out at me, wide-eyed and thoughtful. There flashed through my mind then a most dreadful image. I must have seen it on television, or maybe from a nature magazine, most likely the *National Geographic* – we had a pile of them in the bathroom at home. It was a photograph of a terrified young orang-utan clinging pathetically to the top of a charred tree, the forest all around burnt to the ground.

I turned the page quickly, not wanting to be reminded of it any more. That was when I came across the picture of an elephant walking along a beach, and being ridden by a boy no older than I was. I could not contain my excitement. "Mum," I said, "look at this! They've got elephants, and you can ride them!"

But Mum was fast asleep, and showing no signs whatever of wanting to wake up.

few times, to see my other grandparents. 'Liquorice Allsort', that was what Dad used to call me: "Bit Indonesian, bit Swiss, and a bit Scottish, like me. Best of all worlds, that's what you are, Will," he'd say.

I'd always been very proud of having a mother who didn't look much like my friends' mothers. Her skin was honey brown, smooth and soft, and she had shining black hair. I would have preferred to look like her, but I'm much more like my father, sort of pinkish, with a thatch of thick fair hair, 'like ripe corn', Grandpa called it.

I couldn't help myself. It was something I'd been doing a lot. I kept trying to picture Dad as he was when I last saw him, but all that came into my head was the photo of him I remembered best, the one on top of the piano with him holding the pike. I knew that a memory of a photo isn't a real memory at all. I promised myself again that I would think about Dad more often, however much it hurt me. How else could I keep in touch with him? I wanted to see his smile again, to hear how his voice sounded. Remembering him was the only way. It worried me that if I didn't remember him often, then maybe one day I'd forget him altogether. I needed to remember, but then it troubled me when I did. It was troubling me now, which was why I turned my attention again to the holiday brochure. On every page there seemed to be more elephants. Elephants, I decided, were quite definitely supreme.

And now here I was actually riding one along a beach. I couldn't believe it. I wished then I had Mum's mobile phone on me. I longed to ring Grandpa and tell him what I was doing. I said out loud the first words that came into my head: "You're not going to believe this, Grandpa!" I held my arms high, lifted my face towards the sun, and whooped with joy. The *mahout* turned round and laughed aloud with me.

I think I've loved elephants ever since I was little,

probably ever since my first Babar book. Best of all I
loved the story of 'The Elephant's Child', whose nose

I've always loved any natural history programme, just so
long as there were elephants in it.

And now I was in one, on one, and it was my own
programme! I whooped again, punching the air. High
above me, probably at about 35,000 feet, I thought, flew
a silver dart of a plane, its vapour trail long and straight.
"I was up there," I told the *mahout*. But he didn't seem to
be listening. He was looking out to sea. He seemed
distracted by something. So I told Oona instead. "I was
up there with Mum," I told her, "in a plane just like that
one. And there was an elephant just like you, in the
brochure. Maybe it *was* you."

I remembered how, up in the areoplane, when Mum
woke she leaned over me, brushing my hair away from
my eyes. "I should have cut your hair at Grandma's,"

she said. "I'll do it when we get to the hotel. It's too long. You look like a right ragamuffin."

"Mum," I told her, fixing her with my most determined look. "When we get there, I'm not going to waste time having a stupid haircut, am I? You know what I'm going to do? I'm going to go for a ride on an elephant." I showed her the brochure. "Look at that!"

"Are they safe?"

"Course they are, Mum. Can I?"

"We'll see," she said. "I expect it'll be a bit expensive. We'll have to watch our pennies, you know."

The hotel was right on the beach, and just as beautiful as it had looked in the brochure. And there *was* an elephant too, we were told, that sometimes gave hour-long rides all the way down the beach and back. Every day I looked out for this elephant, but much to my disappointment it was never there. There were compensations enough though. We spent an entire week messing around on the beach, swimming and snorkelling. It was a week filled with endless sun and fun, all in all the very best kind of forgetting. Then on Christmas Day, Mum told me I wasn't getting a

Christmas present this year, I was going to have an elephant ride instead. She'd arranged the whole thing

anyway. There was a wooden rail all round to hold on to. But when the elephant set off, the ride was so smooth that I found I didn't need to hold on at all. I rode along the beach on my throne, looking down on the world around me. I felt like a king up there, or an emperor maybe, or a sultan, except that Mum did rather spoil the illusion, by trotting alongside taking photos of me on her phone to send home to Grandma and Grandpa. I acted up for the camera, waving at it regally. "Hi, Grandpa, hi, Grandma. King Will here. What d'you think of my new tractor then, Grandpa?" I shouted all sorts of nonsense. This was better than I had ever imagined. I felt on top of the world. "Happy up there, Your Majesty?" Mum said, beaming up at me.

"S'all right, I suppose," I told her.

"Mind you keep your hat on, Will, and your shirt. Don't want you getting sunstroke or sunburn, do we?" She went on, and on and on. "And you've got the sun cream, and that bottle of water I gave you, haven't you? It's hot, and it'll get hotter."

"Yes, Mum. I'll be all right, Mum." I was trying to make light of my irritation.

"I'll be fine. Honest, Mum. See you when I get back."

"Don't fall off," she called after me. "Hang on tight. It's a long way down. You will be all right up there, won't you?"

I didn't like her fussing over me, and especially not in front of the *mahout*. I waved her goodbye, waving her away at the same time. "Don't worry, Mum," I told her. "You go and have a swim. It's brill, Mum, just brill." And it was true. I'd never had a ride as brilliant as this, nor as easy as this, nor as high as this. I remembered the donkey on the beach at Weston-super-Mare, with its jerky little steps; and Minky, the Haflinger horse I'd ridden once in Guarda in Switzerland, who used to break into a sudden trot whenever she felt like it, who bumped me up and down

I was afloat. Riding an elephant seemed as natural to me as breathing.

I'd been so wrapped up in my own thoughts, so enthralled by the elephant, and by everything around me, that only now did I think of Mum. I swivelled around in my *howdah* to look for her. I could see there were dozens of swimmers in the sea just below the hotel. I tried to spot her red bikini, or the light blue sarong that Dad had given her, but we'd gone a long way away from them by now, and I couldn't pick her out from among the others. The sea was so still now, it seemed almost unreal. It seemed to me as if it was breathing in, then holding its breath, waiting for something to happen, something fearful. It made me feel suddenly anxious too, which was why I kept turning round now, looking for Mum. I still couldn't see her. I began to feel myself being gripped by a rising panic. I didn't know why, but all I wanted to do was to go back. I wanted to be with her. I had to be sure she was safe.

That was the moment Oona stopped, without any warning at all. She was looking out to sea, her whole body tensed. She was breathing hard, short sharp breaths. Then she lifted her trunk and began trumpeting at the sea, tossing her head as if there was something out there, something that terrified her. The *mahout* was trying to calm her, but she wasn't paying him any attention.

I looked out to sea then, and noticed that the horizon had changed. It looked as if a white line had been drawn across it, separating sea from sky. As I watched I could see that this line was moving ever closer towards us, that the sea was being sucked away, leaving hundreds of fish floundering on the sand. Oona swung round, and before the *mahout* could stop her, she was running towards the trees. In those first few hurried strides I very nearly fell off. I managed to

stay on, only by clinging on tight with both hands to
the rail in front of me. I held on for dear life, as Oona

"No leaves, Oona,
I can't eat leaves"

was being rocked so violently from side to side up in my *howdah* that it was all I could do to avoid being thrown out. I learned fast that I had to keep my head down, that whenever I looked up, there'd be some overhanging branch just ahead of me, waiting to slash and whip and claw at me, or even to knock me off altogether. So I flattened myself face down into the cushion,

closed my eyes, and with all my strength, just hung on, riding the pitch and toss as the elephant blundered through the trees, trumpeting in her terror.

It was the trumpeting I could not stand. It was so loud, so excruciatingly shrill, that it filled my whole head, and the whole forest around me too. I longed to put my hands over my ears, but I could not let go of the rail. The elephant's terror became my terror, and I found myself screaming into the cushion, then biting deep into it, because it was the only way to silence my screams. I'd been to the funfair with Dad, done the Big Dipper and the Waltzer, but that had all been make-believe terror, terror I could laugh at, terror I had to laugh at because Dad was, because everyone was, even though I was frightened out of my wits. But this, this was the real thing, this was life or death – I knew it because Oona was trumpeting it. I had no idea then what she was running from, only that whatever it was must be close behind us and coming after us, and would kill us if it caught up with us.

It wasn't until I felt the sun hot on the back of my neck that I realised we must be out of the dark of the forest. I dared now to lift my head at last and look about me. Oona was charging on through a clearing

so far to fall, too far, and Oona was running on now even faster than before. I was still being tossed about in the *howdah*. I was having to hang on with all my strength so as not to be thrown out. But at least I had discovered a technique for staying in there by this time. Splaying my legs wide behind me, I found I could brace my feet against the rails, and steady myself better. I was beginning to feel a little more secure. I even dared to raise myself up a little, and twist round just for a moment to look behind me to see if the *mahout* had been following us. I'd been hoping against hope all along that he wouldn't be too far behind, that Oona would slow down, and he would catch up, that somehow, some way, he would be able to bring the runaway elephant to a halt. But Oona was showing no sign of slowing down, and the young man was nowhere to be seen.

All this time I was trying to take it all in, to make some sense of it. Everything had happened so fast, and was still happening. All I could be sure of now was that I had no one to turn to, that I was quite on my own. I was being carried off into the forest by a rampaging elephant, who had been spooked by something or someone unknown. Whatever it was had transformed her from a ponderous creature of supreme gentleness and serenity, into a wild raging beast, maddened by terror, who seemingly had only one idea in her head, to get as far from the sea as possible, as fast as possible.

Ahead of us, beyond a clearing, I saw there was a wide rock-strewn stream. I was sure that Oona must have to slow down to cross it — I hoped she might even stop altogether. She did neither. She ran straight down into it, launching herself into the river, so that the water exploded all around us, soaking me to the skin. Once through it and out the other side I saw that there was a long open hill ahead of us before we could reach the tree line again. Only once she was climbing the hill, did

Oona at long last slow to a hurried scuttling walk, her
head nodding vigorously with the effort of it, her great

come, down towards the blue of the ocean beyond.

Only now did I understand what it was that had
spooked the elephant, and why she had kept running
all this time. Everything I was seeing filled me with
horror. A warm shiver of fear crept up my spine and into
the back of my neck. The sea was rearing itself up into
a towering wall of green water that was rushing in
towards the beach, towards the hotel, towards where I
knew Mum was swimming. I could hear it now too, a
distant thunderous roaring. People were running for
their lives up the beach. I couldn't hear their screams,
they were all too far away. But in my head I heard their
terror. I saw boats being picked up like toys, only to
disappear moments later, simply swallowed by the sea.

The great wave didn't curl over and crash along the

beach as I was expecting, but just kept coming, on and on, so fast and so high that it was unreal. It seemed to me like a virtual wave, an impossible wave. There was no beach to be seen any more now, and as I watched I saw that the hotel itself was surrounded entirely by seawater, the first floor already overwhelmed. Everywhere, the water was full of swirling debris: cars, trees, telegraph poles. Entire roofs of houses were being swept along in the torrent like paper hats. I could see there were people caught up in it too, clinging on wherever they could. Any moment now I expected to see the wave crashing through the forest below us, and come rushing up the hill after us. All I knew was that I had to get away, I had to go higher. It was my only chance.

I leaned forward and slapped Oona on the neck, again and again, screaming at her to get going, to go faster. Whether or not she understood I did not know, but to my great relief, I felt her gathering her strength underneath me and then breaking into a lumbering shuffle up the hill and into the forest. All the while I was trying to come to terms with what I'd seen. I was

sure by now that it had to be a tidal wave, a *tsunami*. I'd
seen one in a natural history programme I'd watched

a strange effect on me. I found myself suddenly calmer,
more able to think things through. I now realised that
Oona must have sensed the danger, must have felt it
coming long before she saw it, and long before anyone
else saw it too. I recalled then something the *mahout*
had told me, how she'd been so nervous of swimming in
the sea earlier that morning. Somehow, even then, hours
before, she had felt that something was out there, was on
its way. That must have been why she'd turned and run
when she had, and that was the only reason we had got
this far, the only reason I was still alive, that we were
both still alive.

I could tell Oona was tiring now after all her efforts.
Her breathing was laboured, her steps faltering. I
should have been ready for it, but I wasn't. When Oona

stumbled and nearly fell, I was hurled to one side of the *howdah*, losing my grip almost entirely. I just managed to cling on to the rail with one hand as I was flung over the side. I found myself dangling there, barely able to hang on, as Oona barged and blundered her way through the undergrowth. All I knew was that if I let go, even if I survived the fall with no broken arms or legs, I would not stand a chance on my own without the elephant. I had to hang on. Somehow I swung myself round so that I could cling on with both hands, trying all I could to scrabble up the elephant's side, and haul myself up. But I hadn't the strength to do it. I knew that sooner rather than later, my grip must weaken and I would fall, or that maybe a branch would knock me off as Oona charged on.

I cried out to Oona then, begging her to slow down. Incredibly, she did. Even more miraculously, she came to a stop. Then I saw her trunk come curling round, felt it grasping me by the waist, lifting me up and depositing me in an ungainly heap back in the safety of the *howdah*, where I lay for some moments limp and breathless. Already Oona was on the move again, walking on slowly at first, as if allowing me time to

Only now, as I lay there exhausted in the *howdah* did I really begin to take in the dreadful meaning of everything I had just witnessed. If Mum had been in the sea, or on the beach, or anywhere nearby when the tidal wave swept in, then she must have drowned, along with anyone else in its path. No one caught on the beach or in the sea could possibly have survived the onslaught of such a gigantic wave. No one would have stood a chance. She had told me she was going for a swim. It was almost the last thing she'd said to me. I tried not to believe what this meant, but I had to. Choking back my tears, I kept telling myself that there was at least a possibility that Mum might already have left the beach by the time the *tsunami* struck, that maybe she'd been back in the hotel, and had reached the safety of our room, which was after all on the top floor. If so, she could still be alive. She could be. I so wanted to believe that.

But I only had to think again, and I would know in my heart of hearts, that in all probability she had to have been in the water when the wave struck. I knew how much she loved her swimming, and her snorkelling, how for a whole week now she'd hardly ever been out of the water, how each morning we'd raced each other down the beach and into the water, and how she always swam like a seal, effortless and powerful.

That last thought gave me a sudden lift of hope, that maybe even if she had been caught by the wave she might, just possibly, because she was such a strong swimmer, have been able to swim her way to safety. But I realised that Mum's best chance of survival had to have been the hotel. I tried all I could to persuade myself that she might have gone back to the hotel, to email Grandpa and Grandma again maybe, that she had been up there in our room when the wave came in, that she was alive, that she was not dead and drowned, that she was right now thinking about me, that she'd be looking for me, coming to find me, as soon as she could.

I tried all I could to convince myself that this must

before he went away to the war. God hadn't been listening then, so why should he be listening now? In my despair, I lifted my head and cried out loud, not to God, but to Mum. "Don't die, Mum. Please, Mum. Swim, you've got to keep swimming, you've got to. Don't give up, please don't..."

I was interrupted by the sound of a strange throbbing, distant at first, but suddenly quite close and then right overhead. I could see what it was now – a helicopter, glinting in the sunlight up above the canopy of the trees. I was up on my feet at once, balancing as best I could in the *howdah*, waving my arms wildly and shouting at the top of my voice. But the helicopter was gone within seconds. Just that glimpse though was enough to give me hope again. I knew for sure that they must be looking for survivors, rescuing people, and that one of them could be my mother.

It was at that moment that I made up my mind. Whatever had happened I had to go back to try to find Mum. I yelled at Oona to stop. She didn't pay any attention. I pleaded with her, I shouted at her, I screamed at her, I slapped her neck. Then, when I could see that none of that was doing any good, I tried explaining. "She could be alive!" I told her. "I have to go back. I have to. Turn round, Oona. You must turn round. We have to go back!" But Oona would not be stopped. If anything, she was going faster, blowing and puffing as she went, striding out more purposefully than ever, her trunk swinging, her great ears in full sail. She was going where she was going, and that was that.

I realised then that there was nothing whatsoever I could do to change her mind, and that I had to go where the elephant was going. I had no choice. Understanding this first, then simply accepting it, seemed to enable me to calm down enough to think straight. Hadn't this elephant already saved my life? Hadn't she known exactly what she was doing right

elephant understood things a lot better than I could ever have imagined, that she would not listen, would not turn round and go back, because there was just no point. She knew, as I did, if I was really being honest with myself, that no one could possibly be alive back down there on the coast, and that there was no use any more in pretending otherwise.

As Oona made her way ever onwards and upwards into the forest, I lay there in the *howdah*, on my back now, staring blankly up at the trees above me, consumed utterly by despair, numb with grief and longing. I had no tears left to cry. I could feel the elephant was exhausted, that her stamina was fading fast. She was stumbling more often, breathing harder. She plodded on, tugging at the leaves around her from time to time, feeding as she went. By now though, I no longer cared what she was doing, or where she was going, or even what might happen to me. I did not care about the oppressive humidity of the jungle, nor the flies that settled on me and bit me. I was not frightened in any way by the wild wide eyes of monkeys blinking down at me as I passed by underneath.

After a while I think I became altogether unaware of the passing of time. Night and day were the same for me. I was neither hungry nor thirsty. I drifted often into sleep, but even when I was awake, I was barely more conscious of what was going on around me than when I was in my dreams. I was aware of the moon floating through the treetops, of the buzz and drone of the forest in the heavy heat of the day, of the raucous cacophony of screeching and howling that filled the jungle every night, of the sudden torrential downpours that somehow found their way through the canopy of trees and drenched me to the skin.

None of it bothered me, none of it meant anything to me. I suppose I wasn't even aware enough of my

surroundings
to feel alarmed or
threatened. It did cross my
mind sometimes that I was in a place where there must
be all manner of poisonous snakes and scorpions, and
maybe even tigers too – I remembered, in that holiday
brochure, seeing a photograph of a tiger prowling
through the jungle. I could not have cared less. I was too
lost in misery and grief to be fearful of anything.

I lay like this in my *howdah* for days and nights on

end. I must have drunk from time to time from the bottle of water Mum had given me. I don't really remember doing it, but I must have done, because I woke up once to discover that the bottle was empty. I kept slipping in and out of my dreams, not wanting to wake at all, because I knew that when I did, I'd remember all over again everything that had happened to me and all that it meant: that I had no father, and now no mother, and that I myself would very probably die out here in this jungle. I was so tired and weak and dispirited by this time, that I didn't much mind if I did.

My only comfort was the regular rocking motion of the elephant beneath me. I became so attuned to it, that I always woke whenever it stopped. Often I would hear Oona tugging at the branches then, grunting contentedly as she grazed the forest. And from time to time, whenever she flapped her ears, I'd feel a cooling breeze wafting over me. I came to love those moments. And when I heard the sound of her dung falling, I became accustomed to waiting for the smell of it to reach me. It wasn't unpleasant, no worse anyway than the smells human beings make. In fact, I didn't find it unpleasant at all, it was strangely reassuring. And it made me

then, without thinking about it, I reached out and touched her trunk. As I did so, Oona left it where it was, deliberately it seemed to me, and let me run my fingers along it as she breathed gently on my face. It was like the breath of new life. I knew then that I wasn't alone in the world, that I had a friend, and that I wanted to survive, that I somehow *had* to survive, so I could go back to the coast, and find Mum.

But with this new-found will to live came a sudden unbearable hunger, and with it an overwhelming thirst, a craving for water so strong and all-consuming that I could think of nothing else. I did sometimes manage to grab an overhanging leaf and lick the rainwater from it. Whenever it rained, I'd cup my hands and catch all I could. But there was never enough for me even to begin to quench my thirst, let alone fill my bottle, which was what I knew I had to do if I wanted to survive.

I tried to make Oona understand this every time we came to a stream – and there were enough of those in the jungle – but every time Oona just waded on through and would not stop. I tried whispering gently to her, as I'd seen the *mahout* doing back down on the beach, but it proved to be no use at all. Shouting at her and slapping her neck did not work. Neither did begging or pleading. Stream after stream we crossed, and all I could do each time was gaze longingly down at the rushing water below me that I so longed to be drinking, but was already leaving behind me.

Again and again I seriously considered standing up in the *howdah*, and then throwing myself off into the water when we came to the next stream. I would pick my moment, decide where the water was at its deepest, and leap. I could do it. I could swim well enough – the best in my class at school, better than Charlie or Bart or Tonk. That wasn't my worry. I had other anxieties. If I got it wrong, I could land badly on hidden rocks beneath the surface. I could break a leg, or even my neck. And I knew that rocks weren't the only danger lurking beneath the surface. I was sure there

there waiting for me, even if I had the best of landings, and had the long cold drink I was yearning for, and managed to fill up my water bottle, would Oona stand there and wait for me while I drank? Even if she did, how was I going to climb back up on to her again afterwards into the safety of the *howdah*? Getting on and off this elephant was something I just didn't know how to do on my own. The last time I'd had to do it, days before now, the *mahout* had been there to help me up, but I could not remember for the life of me how he'd got me up there. All that seemed to have happened so long ago now, before the wave came. Mum had been there. Had she helped me up? I couldn't remember. I didn't want to remember.

My longing for food was becoming every bit as

frustrating and urgent as my longing for water. It wasn't as if there wasn't fruit in abundance all around me in the jungle, but none of it was fruit I recognised, and anyway I couldn't get at it. I was looking for bananas – I thought there must be bananas in a jungle – but so far as I could see there were none. There was a small pinky-red fruit, that was shaped something like a banana. But these were always tantalisingly out of reach as I passed by underneath. There were sometimes coconuts, orange, not brown, but anyway they were always growing far too high up. And those that had fallen on the forest floor were of course just as inaccessible to me.

There were plenty of other strange fruits I certainly would have tried, had I been able to get near enough, or quick enough to grab them. But Oona swayed on blithely by, quite oblivious, it seemed, to all my needs. And all this time she was adding insult to injury, because of course Oona could reach out her trunk whenever she felt like it, and with a tug at an overhanging branch, was able to pull it down and eat her fill on the move. Worse still she looked and sounded as if she was enjoying every moment of her feasting. I could only sit there and listen to her great jaws grinding

bent down and bellowed into her ear. I knew it was pointless, but I did it all the same. "Food, Oona! I want food! I want water!" She flapped her ears at me then, as if she was batting away my words like irritant flies. But I kept on at her, whacking her as hard as I could on her neck, on her back, anywhere I could hit her, trying everything and anything to make her listen. "I want to eat, Oona!" I cried. "Fruit. I need fruit. And water, I've got to have water. Please, Oona, please. Can't you understand, Oona? I'll die if I don't have a drink. I'll die!"

In time I discovered that all the bellowing and the whacking and the slapping was hurting me a great deal more than it was hurting her. My hands ached with it. My throat was raw with it. Whatever I said or did, the elephant was not paying me any attention, that was for sure. She simply continued on her wandering way through the jungle, munching nonchalantly as she went, seemingly without a care in the world. I tried everything I knew over and over again. But even as I was doing it, I could see it was useless, that neither sweet-talking, cajoling, begging, whacking, or threatening was ever going to work. This elephant would do what she would do, and that was that. In the end I simply gave up trying.

Exhausted and angry, I lay down in the *howdah*, which I now thought of more as a cage than a throne, and sobbed. Into my head from nowhere came Dad's old joke: "You've got to chill, Will." I said it out loud then, as Dad would have said it. "You've got to chill, Will." Repeating his words time and again was a comfort to me somehow. It was the rhythm of them maybe, or the familiarity. I longed for sleep, because I longed to put out of my mind everything that had happened, all the discomforts I was enduring. It was the only way to forget the gnawing hunger in my stomach, that my tongue was leathery dry, that my throat was parched and sore.

Once, when sleep came at last, I heard Dad's words again in my dreams, and I saw him too. "You've got to

water, trying to reach those outstretched hands before I sank, but the seawater kept coming into my mouth and was choking me. I woke then, suddenly, and sat up spluttering. For a few moments the sunlight blinded me.

The elephant had stopped. There was the sound of rushing water all around me. I sat up. Oona was standing in a river, the water washing over her back and up to her neck and her ears, so that the *howdah* was simply an island now, the river swirling all around. And somehow the *howdah* had worked itself loose. I could feel it shifting sideways off Oona's back, so that some of the cushions were already waterlogged. The river was running fast, but I did not hesitate. This was the chance I'd been waiting for. The shore wasn't that far away. I could make it. If there were crocodiles I did not care. I needed to have water. I had to drink.

I put a foot on the rail and leaped off. Before I knew it I was in the river, and swimming hard for the shore. Just a few strong strokes and I was there. I crouched at the river's edge and drank till I could drink no more, filling myself to bursting. Breathless with drinking now, triumphant with it, I found myself laughing and whooping and slapping the water, filling the forest with my noise, sending thousands of screeching birds flying up out of the trees. "Look at them, Oona!" I cried. "Look!"

All I could see of Oona was her head and her trunk. She seemed to have drifted further down the river, and was right out in the middle now, where the flow was faster. I was quite confident I could swim that far. So without another thought I plunged in. But I found that the current was a great deal stronger out there than I had imagined, and I soon realised that I wasn't going to make it. I just didn't have the strength to sustain the effort. So I had to turn back again, and swim hard for the shore to get myself out of trouble. It was a long swim and I felt myself tiring fast, so it was a huge relief when

then louder and louder as my fears multiplied. My first thought was that Oona must have gone off into the forest and abandoned me. I was sure of it. There could be no other explanation. With panic came hurt. I let her know just what I thought of her. "Go off and leave me then, you great lump, see if I care! I don't need you, you hear me? I don't need you!"

It was then that I caught sight of the *howdah* being swept away downriver towards the rocks, but there was still no sign of Oona. The *howdah* sank as I watched. All I could see of it now were its straps, and then my water bottle and a cushion from the *howdah* bobbing away into the distance. As I stood there I was thinking that the bottle was the last thing Mum had given to me, that and my hat and the sun cream, all of which must have been at the bottom of the river by now with the *howdah*. All I had left was what I stood up in: my shirt and my shorts.

That was when Oona erupted from under the water only a few metres from me, rising up to her full height with the water cascading from her, trunk flailing and splashing. When I got over my surprise, I found myself overwhelmed with sudden joy and relief, all my earlier fury at her instantly forgotten. Oona sank down again into the river, leaving only the great dome of her head and her eyes visible. It seemed to me that she had been playing hide-and-seek with me, that this must be an invitation to come and play with her. It was an invitation I could not resist. As I ran down into the water I wondered how I could ever have doubted her.

Oona was better than any wave machine I had ever known. Whenever she rolled over to loll on her side, she created huge waves that I would dive into. Time and again she'd submerge herself completely, then rear up out of the water, so that it came rushing down her sides like a waterfall, and I would stand there beside her, shrieking under the shower she was giving me. She

swished her trunk at me, sprayed water at me. It was a
performance, a game. I was in fits of laughter the whole

a long galloping piggyback ride, out of the sea and up the
beach towards where Mum was waiting for us. She'd
screamed at us not to drip on her, and we had, as she knew
we would, shaking ourselves like dogs all over her. It had
all been so good. The whole day by the seaside at Weston
came back to me, every detail of it, then all the treasured
memories of home, of Dad and Mum, of all of us together,
of how everything had been before Dad had gone off to
the war, before the tidal wave.

I felt suddenly racked by sadness and guilt. I left
Oona in the river and went to sit on the rocks. All I
could think of was that nothing would ever be the same.
Those days were gone for ever. Mum and Dad were gone
for ever. I would never see them, or hear their voices
ever again. And what had I just been doing? A moment

or two before I'd been having the time of my life, shrieking with laughter as if none of this had ever happened, as if everything was just 'fine and dandy', as Grandpa used to say. Dad was dead, and down on the coast hundreds of people had been drowned by the tidal wave, thousands maybe, Mum among them. How could I have allowed myself to forget them both so quickly? How could I have been laughing when I should have been crying?

But even as I was thinking this, even as I watched Oona wafting her trunk at me from way out in the river, I found I was smiling inside myself, and I knew there was nothing wrong in it, that Mum and Dad wouldn't mind. There was a hummingbird hovering nearby over a flower. She was so tiny, miraculously tiny, and beautiful. And butterflies of all colours were

 chasing each other over the water. That was the moment I felt all the gloom and guilt lifting from me. I was not thinking of the past any more, nor of Mum and Dad. I was thinking that if I had any family at all now, it was Oona. It was a strange idea, I knew that. But the more I began to think about it, the more I believed it was true.

ago at least by now. The only evidence I'd seen of any human existence was the occasional glimpse of a vapour trail high in the sky, thousands of metres above the canopy. No one knew I was here. No one even knew I was alive, so certainly no one would be out looking for me. I had ridden into this jungle on the elephant. If anyone knew the way out, I reckoned, it was her. All I had to do then was to stay with her, and learn to live with her, and I'd be all right. One day sooner or later she'd carry me out of the jungle, just as she'd carried me in.

Meanwhile I had to find some way of communicating with her, of getting her to understand I was starving hungry. I'd heard the *mahout* talking to her down on the beach that morning, but it had been in his language, a language I hadn't understood at all. Oona must have understood, though, otherwise why would he have talked to her as much as he had? So if she had understood his language then she could learn English – it stood to reason. All I had to do was teach her. I remembered how her *mahout* always whispered to her, never raised his voice. I would do the same. Somehow I had to teach her to understand me.

I wasted no time. As soon as Oona came out of the water, I went right up to her. I held her trunk and stroked it as I talked to her, just as the *mahout* had done. As I spoke I was looking her right in the eye, her wise, weepy eye. "Oona," I began, "I know your name, but you don't know mine, do you? You don't know anything about me. So I'd better tell you, hadn't I? Here goes then. I'm Will. I'm nine years old, ten soon, and I live near Salisbury in England, which is a long way away, and that's where I go to school. My Grandpa and Grandma have a farm in Devon, where it's muddy, and he's got a lot of cows, and a tractor, and I go there for holidays. Dad was a soldier and he was killed by a bomb in Iraq because there's a war there, and now I think Mum's dead too, drowned by

Understand? Eat."

I opened my mouth wide, said "aah" several times, sticking my fingers down my throat. Oona looked down at me knowingly from a great height, so knowing that I felt she must be understanding at least the gist of what I was saying. Much encouraged by this I went on. I rubbed my stomach. "Yum, yum. Food. Food." Unblinking, she looked back at me. She was listening, I could tell that much, but now I wasn't so sure she'd understood a single word I'd been saying.

Maybe her eye wasn't knowing after all, simply kind. I just didn't seem to be getting through to her. I had an idea. I decided I'd have to try another tack altogether. I ran off to the edge of the forest, and came back after a while with a long leafy branch I'd torn from a tree. I offered it to her, hoping these might be the kind of leaves she liked. She sniffed at it for a few moments, then curled her trunk around it, ripped off what she wanted and shoved it into her mouth. "Yes, yes, Oona," I cried. "You see? Food. Yum, yum. Me. Me too, I need food. But not leaves, Oona. I can't eat leaves. Fruit. Fruit."

As she chomped and chewed her eyes never left me once, and from somewhere inside her there came a deep groan of contentment. I was hopeful that these were all signs that she understood now, that she was grateful to me for fetching her food, that she would do the same for me. But when she'd finished stuffing in the last of her leaves, all she seemed interested in was exploring my hair and then my ears with her trunk. Exasperated now, I lost my patience. I pushed her away, and shouted up at her. "Can't you understand anything, you stupid elephant? I'm hungry! I just want food! I have to have food!"

I looked around in desperation, and saw there was some kind of red fruit, they looked like huge ripe plums, and they were growing high up in a tree on the far side of the river. "There! Look, Oona! That's what I want. It's too high

she was busy eating again, I discovered that no amount of yelling at her, or leaping up and down, or slapping her leg would distract her. Oona was feeding, and nothing and no one was going to stop her.

I felt my eyes filling with tears. I tried to blink them back. But it was no good – they kept coming anyway. I sat down beside the river, clasped my knees to my chest and let the tears flow. I was sobbing not out of self-pity or grief. There were no thoughts any more of Mum or Dad. I was crying out of fury and frustration, and hunger too. I buried my face in my hands and rocked back and forth, moaning in my misery.

When at last I did look up again, I saw that the

howdah had now become firmly wedged between rocks. It was obvious that there was no possible way I could retrieve it from the river. Without it, I knew I could never ride Oona again. And without Oona how was I ever going to be able to find my way out of this forest, and back to safety? Strangely, it was only now, as I came to understand all this, that I finally stopped crying, and began to calm down and collect my thoughts. If I couldn't ride the elephant, and if she wouldn't find me food, then she couldn't save me. In which case I'd have to search for food myself, fend for myself. I'd have to find another way altogether of saving myself. There had to be a way out of the jungle. There was a way into this place, so there was a way out. I'd just have to find it, that's all.

Only moments later I knew what I had to do. It came to me as I watched the river running by. It was obvious. Why hadn't I thought of it before? I'd follow the river downstream. Didn't rivers always end up sooner or later in the sea? If I followed the river, at least I'd always have water to drink, and I'd be bound to find something to eat on the way – berries, nuts, roots, fish even. I could catch fish. Yes, I'd leave the elephant. That's what I'd do. There and then I made

Tiger, Tiger...

ut the very next moment something happened that changed my mind altogether. I was still sitting there by the river when I felt Oona's trunk touching me softly on the back of my neck. It moved along on my shoulder, snuffling at me, exploring me. I watched it encircling my chest, pulling at me gently, yet insistently. She was turning me round to face her. She stood over me for a

moment, looking down at me, groaning at me reproachfully, as if she knew I'd been doubting her, as if she realised I'd been thinking of leaving her.

She began to lower herself down on to her front knees. At first I thought she was probably tired after all her exertions in the river, and was just going to lie down beside me and rest. And indeed that's what she did, but it soon became apparent to me that this wasn't because she was tired at all. She was reaching out her trunk again towards me, curling it round my waist and then drawing me in towards her. It took a while for me to understand why she was doing this.

Then I knew what she was trying to tell me. There could be no doubt about it. This had to be an invitation to climb up. She was helping me all the way, nudging me, lifting me, supporting me until I found myself astride her neck, sitting there behind the twin domes of her head. Until now I had only really thought she had one dome on the top of her head, but now it was clear to me there were two.

Oona heaved herself up then, her trunk steadying me all the while, until she was standing upright again on all fours. But without the *howdah* there was no rail for me to hold. I panicked, and threw myself forward on her

hard with my knees and my heels.

But I found my legs were too short and splayed too wide apart, so that any real grip was impossible. If Oona's trunk wasn't there to hold on to, if she took it away – and sooner or later I knew she'd have to – I could see I was going to have to rely almost entirely on balance to prevent myself from falling off. I really did not know if I could stay on her once she began to move. And if she started to run, then I knew I'd be in real trouble.

But to my great relief, when Oona did begin to walk on up into the jungle she moved only slowly. She took me on a gentle wander, meandering through the trees, and all the time her trunk was there for me to hang on to. I hung on tight with two hands, because at first, even though she was going so slowly, every step she took was nerve-racking for me.

But after a while, when I found I was still up there, that I hadn't fallen off, I began to feel my confidence growing. I was already learning how to attune my balance to the rhythm and sway of Oona's walk. And what I was beginning to sense as well, was that she was adjusting her walk to me all the time, that she was teaching me, helping me, that she would not let me fall. In no time at all I found I was more relaxed, that I was enjoying riding her again. I was beginning to look around me, at the parrots flying through the forest, cawing at me, squawking, cackling, then at the dizzying height of the trees, and the sunlight filtering through.

It wasn't long before I trusted myself enough to take one hand off her trunk, and for a few moments even two. She left her trunk there for me all the same, which was just as well, because my new-found bravado was more fragile than I thought. More than once, when I became too overconfident, my balance failed me, and I did come very close to falling off. But each time this happened and I didn't fall, it gave me new self-belief, that I could

hours passed, I began to feel an irresistible weakness coming over me. I could feel that the little strength I had left was fast draining away. I forced myself to concentrate harder, told myself that I mustn't loosen my grip on Oona's trunk. But my head was swimming now. I felt I might lose consciousness and slip off at any moment. Sometimes I couldn't work out whether I was daydreaming or sleeping. I kept imagining I was in the aeroplane with Mum, that I was asleep beside her and dreaming I was riding on an elephant along a sandy beach, with Mum running alongside taking photographs of me, and telling me to smile and wave.

Time and again I came out of my daydream to discover that it was only partly true. I was riding on an elephant, but Mum was not with me. I was in a jungle not on a beach, and I kept wondering where Mum was. I called for her, but she never answered. I was so weak by now that I could barely sit upright at all. I have no idea how long I rode up there in and out of my dreams, only that the sun was above me sometimes and then the moon, that there was rain, and heat, and flies. But always Oona's trunk would be round me, holding me up there.

Then once when I woke, there was suddenly no trunk to hold me steady, no trunk to cling to. Oona wasn't walking any more. She was standing still, her ears wafting slowly. With no trunk to hold on to, I took fright at once. I gripped tight with my knees and legs, threw myself forward on to her neck and clung there. It was some moments before I had the nerve to sit up again, and look to see what Oona was doing. All I could see at first was the blinding glare of the sun shafting through the canopy above.

Then I saw them. Figs. Dozens of them, hundreds of them, hanging there above us, and Oona's trunk was reaching out to wrap itself around a branch and pull it down towards me. Food, food at last! Oona had understood.

my best to keep up, peeling the next one at the same time as I was trying to finish eating the one before, and while still trying to swallow the one before that. I was stuffing them in. Oona seemed quite happy to reach up and pull down yet another fig-laden branch for me whenever I reminded her, and this I did often, again and again until the time came when I knew I could not eat any more.

But Oona's appetite for figs was insatiable. I looked on in awe and admiration as she stripped the tree of the last reachable fruit. Clearly this had been just a starter course for her, because when she'd done with the figs, she set about stripping a nearby tree of its leaves and twigs as well – they all went into the munching machine together. There was a rhythm about her eating that I found almost musical: from tree to trunk to mouth, from tree to trunk to mouth, accompanied all the while by the sound of those great grinding jaws, and a constant groaning drone of contentment from somewhere hollow deep inside her.

All of this did go on for rather a long time, long after I had ceased to find it at all fascinating. Soon I had more urgent concerns. I really did need to get down. I couldn't put it off for much longer. I kept telling her I needed to go 'to the bathroom', as Grandma had always insisted I called it. But Oona wasn't at all interested in what I wanted because Oona was eating, and I knew by now that nothing was going to interrupt that, that I was in for a very long wait, and there wasn't a thing I could do about it, except to try to think of something else. But that didn't work either. Only when she had eaten her fill did she at last pay me some attention, and it was only just in time.

This was one of the reasons why, from then on, as the days passed, and the weeks, as the rains came and went, I chose more and more not to ride up on Oona, but instead to walk alongside her, particularly when the jungle was not too dense around us. Sometimes it looked quite impenetrable, and then I always rode, because

tor her. Toucans flew overhead from tree to tree above us, an escort in scarlet uniforms and yellow bills. Bright blue peacocks strutted close by, sounding out their raucous fanfare.

In fact the whole jungle, it seemed to me, was welcoming her, celebrating her arrival. Sometimes she would trumpet back her response, in appreciation perhaps, or simply to announce her arrival as she went. Then one day, high, high above us, swinging through the branches of the forest canopy, I saw the dark and distant shape of my first orang-utan, watching us, following us, I thought, keeping his distance.

Like this orang-utan, so many of the forest creatures looked down from a respectful distance, obviously intrigued by this awesome giant that was meandering majestically through their world. But they seemed to understand that her presence among them was entirely benign, that she posed no threat whatever. None of them ran away at our approach. Only the insects — and these came in all sizes and colours and shapes, but all of them, it seemed to me, with an insatiable appetite for blood, whether elephant or human — showed Oona no respect whatsoever. And that was another reason why I so often decided to go on foot, because in the end I found that the further I was from Oona, the less the flies bothered me. But there was a downside to this.

Leeches.

I soon discovered that the more I walked, the more exposed to leeches I became. They would attach themselves to me without my knowing it, mostly to my legs, where they would feed on me surreptitiously, until I discovered them. I learned to loathe these hideous, blood-sucking slugs more than anything in the forest, more even than the flies. They were drinking me alive. I could see my blood pulsating inside them. It disgusted me to have to look at them, and it was worse still to have to deal with them, but I had to, every time I prised them off – I found a sharp-edged stone was the best leech remover. I had to force myself to do it, sometimes

trouble. So to walk alongside her was all the snake protection I needed. Even the crocodiles kept their distance. But I did notice that Oona took no liberties with crocodiles. There was mutual respect here. She would always pause, and wait for me to get up and ride on her, whenever we came to a river or a swamp. I needed little persuasion. I recognised by now that Oona knew well enough what was safe for me, and what was not. I had come to trust her judgement implicitly.

As we wandered on ever further, ever deeper into the jungle, the rains came down more and more often, not rain as I had known back on the farm in England, but sudden and, thunderous on the canopy of leaves above me, so loud that the noise of it drowned out all the whooping and whirring of the forest. When it came, both Oona and I were instantly soaked to the skin. We might have been shielded to some extent, by the dense canopy above us, from the full force of each downpour. But if we ever emerged into the smallest of clearings, the rain fell on us with such violence that it hurt. Sometimes it felt more like warm hailstones than rain. In time, I found out that the only effective protection from the ferocity of storms like these was to tear off a great leaf from a tree and hold it above my head like an umbrella. I felt quite clever doing it too. I once told Oona, "I'd do the same for you, Oona, only there isn't a leaf big enough, is there?"

I talked to her more and more often now. My chatter became a kind of running commentary, a mishmash of all my observations and feelings, jokes even, whatever came into my head at the time. I found that talking to Oona came to me quite naturally. I felt that she liked me to talk, liked the sound of my voice, that she was listening because she liked me to be there, because we had become friends, proper friends who trusted one another.

There was a lot I had come to love and respect about this elephant, especially how nothing seemed to perturb

at all. She ambled on through the forest, aware of every creature around her, and utterly unafraid. I did think sometimes that this might be because her mind was always on her stomach.

Oona was on a perpetual quest for food, browsing constantly as she went, whether in the midst of a downpour or not, her trunk reaching out to explore the branches ahead of her, searching out the most succulent leaves, the ripest fruit. If the fruit on a likely looking tree was too high and inaccessible she'd simply push the tree over, or pull a branch down and break it off. If a fruit was too hard, she'd seem to know how to crack it open, or break it apart, with her trunk or her teeth. No fruit was ever too awkward for her. I loved to watch her trunk at work, almost, it seemed to me, with a mind of its own. I wondered at how skilful and delicate an instrument it could be, how powerful, how sensitive, how infinitely manoeuvrable.

Downpours in the jungle could go on for days at a time, I discovered, and they could stop as suddenly as they had begun. For me this moment always came as a great and welcome relief, leaving the jungle steaming and dripping around us, and slowly finding its musical voice again, all the whooping and howling and croaking, joining together in unison to celebrate the end of the storm. This jungle chorus was so familiar to me by now that I missed it when it was not there filling my head. I felt that the forest was soaking up its own music, as well as all the rain that had fallen, as if it were a living, breathing sponge. There were times now when I thought that in some strange way I was being soaked up too, that I was fast becoming a part of this gigantic, all-consuming sponge.

It was easier to talk to Oona when I was not competing with the thunder of rain. I had long since abandoned any idea of teaching Oona some understanding of English, because I had come to

realise as time passed that Oona did not need to know
exactly what words meant, but that she understood

how to climb on to her neck, how to ride her, and feel
safe about it too?

The more I thought about it, the more I believed
that she knew absolutely which fruit was right for me to
eat, and therefore which fruit was not, and maybe what
water I could drink too. She had been looking after me
all along, not because I'd told her what to do or how to
do it, and certainly not because she understood my
language. This elephant was knowing. She was
intelligent, thoughtful, and deeply sensitive to my
needs. It was becoming clearer to me with every day
that there was nothing whatsoever I could teach her, that
it was in fact she who was the teacher here, not me.

My actual words in themselves might have meant
little to her, but I knew for sure that she was listening,

and that she understood the feeling behind them, the gist of what I was telling her. That was enough for me. Besides, I needed someone to talk to. And I have to admit that I talked to her also because I liked to hear the sound of my own voice in this place. Everyone else had their voice in the jungle, so why shouldn't I have mine? I knew I must be repeating myself all the time, but Oona didn't seem to mind that. In those early days in the forest I would keep coming back again and again to what it was that still troubled me most, despite every attempt to put it out of my mind. It helped me to speak it out, to have someone to tell.

I'd always begin my monologues in much the same way: "Oona, are you listening?" Even as I was saying this, I knew it was a silly thing to say, because she was always listening. "I've been thinking a lot, trying to sort things out in my mind, you know? There's no point in trying to find my way back – I can see that now. What would I go back for anyway? Mum's not there. I still keep hoping she might be, but I know she's not. And Dad's not there. I keep thinking about them and I mustn't. I keep talking to you about them, and I mustn't.

It's like Grandpa said – I've just got to put a plaster over it, and it'll get better. He was right about that, Oona:

understood about death, and about grief too. "You know when I'm really sad and down in the dumps, Oona, don't you? I don't talk to you then, do I? That's because I'm crying inside, and you can't talk when you're crying. When I'm like that I don't care whether I live or die. But I have to care, don't I? Because if you don't, you just give up and die. So that's why I have to keep telling myself, and telling you, that I've got you instead. You're my family now, Oona. My home isn't Salisbury any more, or down on the farm with Grandpa and Grandma in Devon. It's here in the jungle with you. Wherever you take me, that'll be my home. Wherever you go, I'll go. And I won't mind where that is, honest, just so long as you feed me lots of figs, and just so long as you don't ever leave me. You and me, Oona, we've got to stick together, right? Promise? Love you, Oona." That's more or less how I'd ramble on to her.

Above all I always wanted to remind her that I loved her. I'd try to remember to tell her that last thing at night before I went off to sleep. Mum had always told me the same thing at bedtime; Dad too, when he was home. I always loved them saying it. And now it comforted me to be saying it to Oona each night, helped me to put the past behind me, and to come to terms with my new life in the jungle with Oona.

Of course I didn't expect any kind of response from her to anything I'd said. I did think sometimes, that an occasional, 'Love you too,' would have been nice. But it never happened. There was one time though, when she did reply, in a sort of a way, in a most surprising way actually. I'd just said my 'goodnight, love you', when she let out one of the longest, loudest farts I had ever heard in all my life. I'd known her long enough by now to know she was a frequent farter, but this particular one was truly the most magnificent fart of all farts, and musical too, one that seemed to go on and on interminably. I could hear my own giggling echoing through the trees

long after I'd finished. I remember I'd always giggled
with Bart and Tonk and Charlie when someone let off in

There wasn't any real need to stop myself either
when my laughter turned to tears, as it so often had done
since I'd been in the jungle with Oona. I could tell it
upset her when I cried, so I did my best not to. I
promised her so often that I wouldn't cry again, but it
was a promise I was still struggling to keep. I went on
promising her all the same, because I knew that one day
if I promised it often enough, it would help me to make
it happen. "I'm not going to cry, Oona." I'd hold her
trunk between my hands, close my eyes, and tell her yet
again. "I'm not going to think of them. I mean it this
time. I really mean it. I promise. I promise. I promise."

Every night during those early times with Oona, I
tried to keep that promise, and there were many nights
when I failed. There were no weeks and months for me

any more, not in this place, only days, and the long long nights. Whenever I saw a glimpse of the moon through the trees above, I'd think about where I'd seen it before, through the window at home, out camping with Dad. It was these nights I hated most, for it was then that, however much I tried, the old griefs would come welling up inside me again. All I could do then was give myself up to tears. In some strange way though, I found the discomfort of having to sleep rough in the jungle each night did help to distract me from the sadnesses I was trying so hard to forget. In the first place, I had to concentrate all my mind on making myself comfortable, on collecting and piling up a bed of leaves to lie on, always close enough to Oona, but not so close that I'd have to share her flies.

I had learned from bitter experience by now that the damp of the ant-infested, leech-infested forest floor was no place to spend a night. So I did spend a lot of time and trouble every night making myself a substantial nest of leaves, preferably off the damp of the forest floor, on some nearby rock if possible. But even so, I could never get to sleep easily. I couldn't forget the jungle

with. Here the full orchestra of the jungle, along with my fears, and my memories, as well as the insects, did their very best to prevent me from sleeping. Every night was a battle that had to be won before sleep would come, and every night it was Oona who helped me win it.

Time and time again I found that it was only when my thoughts turned to Oona that I could begin to forget everything else. It was so dark at nights that I often could not see her even though she was always near. I could always hear her though, and that was all the reassurance I needed. I'd listen to her rumbling away, groaning and grunting softly. It was like a lullaby to me. Sometimes, when she came close enough, I could feel her ears wafting away the insects and fanning me gently, reminding me she was there when I was feeling at my very lowest. Somehow she seemed to know when that was, when she was needed most. I'd feel her breath warm my cheek and the soft tip of her trunk checking me out. Then I could relax, then I could sleep. Stuff everything, I thought, stuff all the sadness, stuff the leeches. I had Oona. In the morning everything would be fine again.

the waxing and waning of the moon told me that much. These were days and months that had changed me utterly, my whole being, my whole reason for living. Back at home, everything I'd done, I'd done for some specific reason and purpose. When I watched a DVD it was to see what would happen at the end. I used to get up at half past seven in the morning in order to go to school, in order to get there on time, because if I didn't I was in trouble. And when I got to school, I would maybe do a test in order to show I had learned what I was supposed to have learned. Back at home I would have to wash my hands before a meal, because I was told to, because they had to be clean, so that I wouldn't catch germs and get ill. When I went on a journey, it was always in order to arrive somewhere, at the library perhaps, at the doctor's, at the seaside, at the farm. Every hour of every day, everything I ever did seemed to have a different purpose. Life was full of endless purposes.

Here in the jungle there was only one simple purpose, and it was the same every day: to stay alive. Oona and I were travelling, not to get from one place to another, not to arrive, but only to find food and water, only to survive. It was a different way of being altogether, a new and uncomplicated kind of existence. And with it came a growing familiarity with the jungle around me, the world I now depended on. I was beginning to feel a kinship with this world, such as I had never known before. I was no longer a stranger in this place.

I was coming to believe more and more that the jungle was where I truly belonged, that I was becoming a part of it, that this new rhythm of life was the same for me as it was for every other creature in the jungle, from the leeches on the forest floor that I so loathed, to that distant, shadowy orang-utan I loved to watch swinging majestically above us high in the trees, so unlike the

sad little creature I'd seen in that magazine back home,
lost and bewildered in the burned-out wasteland of his

And even to look at I wasn't the same person any
more. From time to time I'd catch sight of myself when I
went down to fish in a river or to have a drink. The boy I
saw staring back at me hardly resembled the same boy
who had been carried off on Oona's back all that time
ago. My shirt had long since been abandoned, ripped
apart and shredded by the jungle, so all I had left were
my tattered shorts. The buttons had mostly come off by
now. So that they wouldn't fall off, I tied them up as best
I could through the belt loops with jungle twine. I still
had to keep hitching them up all the time, but it worked
well enough, mostly. I was a mess. My hair hung down
almost to my shoulders, and was no longer the colour of
ripe corn, but was bleached almost white now – my
eyebrows too. And my skin was nut brown, with sun or

dirt or both. I looked as I felt, like someone else altogether.

It was this transformation, I think, that softened the pain of my grieving and stopped my tears altogether. I was able to believe now that everything before the tidal wave had happened to another boy, a different boy, the pink one, the one who went off to school every day with Tonk and Bart and Charlie, who went for holidays down to the farm in Devon, who drove Grandpa's tractor, and supported Chelsea and ate pies and crisps before the match, whose Mum and Dad were dead now. That was another boy, in another time, in another world. I was a wild boy now, with calloused hands, with the bottom of my feet as hard as leather, a boy of the jungle, and Oona was all the friends and family I had, all I needed. She was my teacher too, and she taught only by example. From her I was slowly learning to live with the heat and humidity of the jungle, and even with the insects too. Like her, I simply devised a better way of dealing with them. I didn't curse them or dread them so much, but instead tried to accept them as Oona did. It wasn't always easy, but I tried.

I learned from her that in the jungle everything and everyone has its place, that to survive you need to find

let it pass. If a crocodile is basking on a river bank, mouth open, watching you, it means: this is my place, take care, keep out of my way. So much in the jungle depends on respecting the space of others. Some creatures eat one another – leeches ate me for a start – but most are fruit eaters, or insect eaters, or frog eaters, and just want to avoid trouble.

And one of the best ways of avoiding trouble, I was discovering, was being ready for it, being aware. See it coming, hear it coming, and most importantly of all, feel it coming. As Oona had shown me so often, she could do this supremely well. I really did have the very best of teachers.

But it wasn't Oona who taught me to fish. I had Dad to thank for that. It was seeing a plastic bag caught up on a branch and dangling in a river that reminded me of something he'd taught me once. He never told me much about the things he did in the army – he didn't seem to want to talk about it. But he did teach me how to catch fish if you were living off the land, with no rod and no line. He used trousers. He showed me. He tied both the legs of some old jeans with twine from a tree, ran more twine through the belt loops, and then strung them up to a branch overhanging the river, so that the jeans were submerged in the water. Ballooned by the current, they acted like a net, so that any passing fish swam in. I remember thinking how brilliant that was – even though Dad never actually caught a fish, just lots of creepy crawlies. I tried it again and again now, using my shorts. It didn't work the first time, nor the second. But the third time, I caught a fish. It was tiny, but it was a fish. I killed it, scraped off the scales with my teeth and ate it raw. Nothing had ever tasted so good to me as that fish. From then on I caught fish whenever I could.

It made a change from fruit.

Fruit had kept me alive. I could shin up a tree for

bananas, but it was the orange coconuts that were the real life savers for me. Sometimes Oona would knock

than any other food.

I was becoming more resourceful with every day, working out for myself better ways of living, safer ways, more comfortable ways. From time to time, when I couldn't find a convenient rock, I had taken to spending my nights now in a tree. I'd climb up a hanging vine – I'd become quite good at this – make myself a nest of twigs and leaves up in among the branches, bending them in, weaving them into a bed, and then lie down to sleep, with Oona below me nearby. It took a while to build, but it was worth it. There were fewer insects up there to bite me, fewer leeches to eat me. It provided shelter from the rain, and anyway it was a whole lot more comfortable than bedding down on the forest floor, and safer too.

I woke one morning up in a tree to discover the tip of Oona's trunk touching my shoulder. She was just below me, grunting and swaying impatiently from side to side, a sure sign, I knew, that she wanted to be on her way. Perhaps the food had run out where she was, or maybe she was thirsty. Whatever it was, when Oona wanted to go, I didn't argue. There was an urgency about her swaying that morning. She clearly wanted me to hurry. There was a wary look in her eye too that made me think at once there might be something worrying her, that she felt there might be some danger nearby. I let myself down from my nest of leaves and on to her neck.

"What is it, Oona?" I said. "What's the matter?"

She set off at once, and much faster than usual. She was looking about her all the while, and tossing her head. She wasn't on the lookout for food, I was sure of that. She began to trumpet then, and that was when I knew for sure that something was wrong, that there really was something out there in the jungle that was alarming her. We were being watched. I could feel it. Whatever it was, was nearby, and whatever it was, was dangerous. I was scanning the forest now, looking for any sign of movement. A toucan flew off, a sudden flash

but I couldn't see him. The jungle was agitated, unsettled, on edge, watching. I had known it like this once or twice before, a sudden and inexplicable eruption of jungle panic. But Oona had never been worried then. Nothing had ever happened – it had always been a false alarm. This time, something did happen, and when it did, it happened quite suddenly.

I saw a shadow moving through the trees ahead of us. The shadow came into the light, flickered into a flame of orange fire, and became a tiger. He came padding out of the forest on to the trail, stopped and turned to look up at us, hissing at us repeatedly, showing his teeth. Oona trumpeted again, and wheeled round to face him, trunk raised, ears displayed. Then in a moment, all was still. Elephant and tiger stood there

eying one another for several minutes, but without ever

below me now, gazing up at me out of unblinking amber eyes, magnificent, awesome, terrifying. I went cold all over. I could hear my heart pounding in my ears. I could feel the hairs standing up on the back of my neck. I dared not breathe, but sat rigid on Oona's neck, clenching myself all over from my jaws to my fists, holding myself tight together, doing all I could not to betray my fear. I could smell the tiger's breath as he panted. I could see the pink of his lolling tongue. He was that close. One spring and I knew that would be the end of me. The tiger's twitching tail told me that it was very likely he was thinking just the same thing.

I did not look directly back into the tiger's eye – I knew better than to do that with any animal by now. In fact I tried all I could, as the tiger circled us, not to look at him at all, in case my courage failed me completely. I didn't trust myself to stay brave, which was why in the end I began to play out a fantasy game between myself and the tiger. I made myself believe that this tiger, that was only a couple of metres below me now, was not real at all, but only virtual, virtual like the lion in *The Lion, the Witch and the Wardrobe*, virtual like the polar bear in *The Golden Compass*, an imagined lion, an imagined polar bear. The tiger looking up at me was still frightening, still terrifying, but this was now an imagined terror that I was living through, the kind I could almost enjoy because I knew the fear was imagined too, only virtual, virtual like the tiger. It was pure self-deception, I knew it was. It may have been a ridiculous ruse, but it worked.

When the tiger came too close for comfort, Oona let him know, not by trumpeting at him, not by charging him. All she did to warn him off was to toss her head at him, swinging her trunk a little, and swishing her tail. It was enough. The tiger licked his whiskers, hissed up at us again a few times to show his displeasure, twitched his tail and padded off back into the jungle, his dignity

and Oona's dignity intact. Oona rumbled inside herself,
in triumph, I thought, waved her ears, and then walked

on the whole planet, that's what you are. You just faced
down the best killing machine in the world, and sent
him on his way. And now all you can think of is eating
again. You are something else, you know that? You're
really something else."

She farted again then, only gently, but it was enough
to release all my pent-up fear, and convert it into
laughter, laughter that rang out through the trees. The
gibbons were laughing back at me now, the toucans too,
and soon the whole forest was loud with laughter all
around us.

A feast of figs

or days after that first encounter with the tiger, I rarely strayed further than a metre or so from Oona's side, insects or no insects. I no longer wandered on ahead of her as I had taken to doing so often. I played it safe, riding up there on Oona's neck where I knew I was out of danger, and from where I had a much better view and an early warning of everything going on around me. At

nights I climbed a lot higher into the trees than ever before to build my nest of leaves and branches, and Oona would stay right below whichever tree I'd chosen all night long, on lookout. I slept lightly, alert to the slightest rustle, half listening for him all the time.

But as time passed, and there was no sign or sighting of the tiger, I grew less anxious. I still slept high in the trees every night, as high as I dared to climb, and I hardly ever went anywhere on foot now, but that wasn't entirely because of the tiger. I had noticed that all the monkeys around me rarely came down on to the forest floor. It seemed sensible to follow their example, to keep out of harm's way. For me, as for them, the tiger was simply one of the many dangers lurking in the darkness of the jungle. Even by day, it was more often than not a dark place, a place of deep shadows, cut off as it was almost altogether from sunlight by the thick canopy of the trees above. *Better to be safe than sorry*, I thought. Sleep high, stay high.

In a strange way I actually found myself missing the tiger. I kept hoping I would see him again. More than that, I was even longing for it. As I lay there one night in my sleeping nest, I kept remembering the tiger poster

to learn it by heart for homework, but I could only ever manage to recite the first verse before drying up. I couldn't remember even that much now, but the first couple of lines did come back to me, and I spoke them out loud again and again, because I thought it sounded so much how the tiger had looked to me, as if the poet had been there and seen him with me. And anyway, I thought Oona would like to hear it.

"'Tyger Tyger burning bright, in the forests of the night. What immortal hand or eye could frame thy fearful symmetry?'"

I got a deep rumble of appreciation from down below, and I knew she'd be smiling away down there in the darkness. I wished now that I had learned it better so that I could have recited the rest of it for her. As I went to sleep that night, I tried to see the words again as they were printed on the poster, but all I could visualise were snatches of lines, bits and pieces. However, the harder I tried, the more I was remembering. I hoped it was all there somewhere, deep in my memory, lost for the moment, but not entirely forgotten.

When we did see the tiger again, it turned out to be in no sense a repetition of the earlier stand-off. There was no hissing this time, no trumpeting. This time he came wandering on to the track in front of us, and looked back at us over his shoulder, as if to say: "Are you going my way? That's fine by me." I was tingling with apprehension and excitement, and I could feel that Oona remained wary too. She did not show it though. As she walked on she never broke the rhythm of her stride. We followed the tiger through the jungle for most of that morning.

After a while, I began to relax, more and more sure all the time that the tiger was not doing this because he wanted to eat me. It was simply because he liked the company. There could be no other explanation. He

So at ease did I become that day with our new travelling companion that I felt I might even try to talk to him. But then I didn't seem to know what I should say. I mean, what do you say to a tiger? It was so important to say the right thing, but I couldn't find the right words. So I decided in the end to recite the poem for him – the bits I could remember anyway – because I felt the words were full of wonder and respect, and I hoped he might pick up on that. Somehow – and to be honest, I have no idea how – when I began to recite the poem this time, every line, then every verse, all of it, just flowed from my memory, almost as if the poet was inside my head and speaking it out for me, maybe because he too knew this was the right moment for his poem to be heard, that this listener was the one he'd written it for, the listener who mattered to him more than any other. I remembered his name then, suddenly. Blake, William Blake. It said so on the poster, right at the bottom.

"Tyger Tyger burning bright, in the forests of the night.
   What immortal hand or eye could frame thy fearful symmetry."

As I spoke it, I so wanted the tiger to listen to me. I was encouraged by his ears, that were turning constantly, backwards, forwards, this way and that. I recited the poem again, projecting my voice this time, so that the tiger should be in no doubt that the poem had been written just for him, and that I was reciting it just for him too. I was so pleased with myself for remembering it. I recited the poem over and over again, to prove to myself that I really could do it, and to drum it into my brain so that I would never be able to forget it.

Just as I began it for the umpteenth time, the tiger stopped in his tracks, and turned to look up at me. At that moment I had no doubt whatsoever that he had

sprang lightly away into the shadows of the trees, and vanished. I could tell at once, that unlike me, Oona was glad to see the back of him. She was much more at ease now that we were on our own again.

That walk through the jungle proved to be the longest the tiger ever stayed with us, the longest he hung around. He did show himself to us several times more after that, just to remind us he was still there, I thought, just so we didn't forget him. But I needed no reminding, and I certainly couldn't forget him. I felt his presence about us all the time. I heard him roaring at night too, heard the hullabaloo of alarm he created in the forest wherever he went.

Then one morning we came across him swimming in a jungle pool. I was sure he knew we were coming, that he'd been waiting for us. Oona watched him for a while from the bank, but when there was water to be drunk and mud to wallow in, and no crocodiles, Oona never hesitated for long, not even for a tiger. Keeping a safe distance from him, she lumbered into the water, and was soon indulging in all her usual flamboyant water sports, creating as much noise and kerfuffle as she could, slapping her trunk into the water and hosing herself down.

I knew what was going on here. Very deliberately, very ostentatiously, she was claiming the pool. So, in the same spirit, I joined in. I leaped off her back with a great whoop, and cannonballed into the river. The tiger clearly did not appreciate this disruption to his tranquil morning swim. In the end he swam away to the far bank where he climbed out on to a rock, shook himself dry and stretched himself out in the sun, ignoring us both. I showed off for him, diving underwater, disappearing for several moments and then appearing elsewhere.

Then I thought I'd show the tiger my best trick of all. With Oona standing in deep water, I clambered up her trunk, stood on her back, balanced myself, punched the air, yelling "Up the Blues", and then leaped off. When

[...illegible, obscured text...]

that made me think that this tiger was pretending. He may not have been fascinated by all our frolicking, but he did stay. I had the distinct impression that even if he wasn't going to show it, he liked having us there, he was enjoying our company – at a distance. I was busy skimming stones, I remember, telling Oona how Dad had taught me to do it, how the secret of success was to find a flat stone, when I saw the tiger get up, and give us a long look. Then with a twitch of his tail, he padded across the rocks, sprang down on to the beach, and disappeared into the jungle.

But this wasn't the last time I saw him, because after that I saw him in my dreams almost every night. By day

I'd look for him everywhere and never see him, but by night he'd be there padding through my dreams, down on the farm in Devon maybe, having tea in the kitchen with us, or in the classroom at school gazing up at the poster of himself and reading the poem, or we'd be back in the jungle together, and I would be there walking alongside Oona and the tiger with my hand resting on his neck, and he'd be like a brother to me. And once, he was even walking with me and Oona and Dad down the Fulham Road on the way to Stamford Bridge to watch Chelsea play. The four of us walked out on to the pitch, and there were 40,000 fans cheering us. That was far and away the most amazing dream I'd ever had in all my life. I always wanted to dream it again. But I never could.

I told Oona about it one day, the day I found the tennis ball. In order to explain the dream better to her, I had to remind her first about how I used to go to matches at Chelsea with Dad, and all about the pork pies and the crisps, about how Mum hated us eating 'all that rot' as she called it. I knew I must have told Oona everything about myself several times over by now. So it certainly couldn't

rolling in it. Rolling in mud was Oona's ecstasy time, but I hated it when she had her mud baths because she would stay smelly and then dusty for days afterwards. I knew she loved mud, and that she needed mud to keep her cool, that it kept the parasites away; but as I pointed out to her, often, it was me who had to sit on her when she was smelly, and the more smelly she was the more she attracted the insects. I ticked her off every time she did it – not that it did any good.

It was at times like that, smelly times, that I preferred to run on ahead of her. With no more sightings of the tiger for a while now, I'd taken to doing this more and more, straying further and further ahead. Just as I had sensed the tiger's presence before, even when I couldn't see him, now I sensed his absence. He was gone, I was sure of it. Anyway, nothing frightened me that much any more about this place, not even the prospect of meeting the tiger face to face again. I had other company – that orang-utan still shadowed us from high in the branches. He never came closer, but when he wanted to let us know he was there, he would blunder about, deliberately I thought, and shake the branches at us. I was beginning to think of him now

a challenge I relished. I could climb more swiftly now, gripping instinctively with my toes as well as with my fingers, and not looking down. I'd climbed trees a lot, back on the farm in Devon, but always nervously – to be honest, I'd never much liked heights.

But heights didn't bother me now, not any more. And when I ran, there was a new spring in my legs, an agility and a balance that had never been there. Everything came easier to me. I wouldn't scramble over a fallen tree trunk as I had before, I would leap it like a deer. I bounded and vaulted and hurdled with consummate ease. I was revelling in my new-found speed and stamina. I felt I could run all day now and never get tired. So when Oona was covered in mud from her wallowing, and stinking to high heaven, I was more than happy to run on ahead for ever if I had to.

But where the trees grew dense and impenetrable around us as they often did, then whether Oona was stinking or not, I'd have to sit up there on Oona's neck and put up with it, because I knew that for me this was the only way through the jungle. Oona could barge and trample her way through the jungle when it was like this. I couldn't. Of course she'd always take the easy route along a jungle trail if there was one. But if not, or if she was after particularly succulent fruit or leaves, then she'd just shove her way in and keep going, tearing aside the undergrowth with her trunk, or simply crushing it with her great bulk and treading it underfoot.

When the forest was this dense it was inevitably an uncomfortable ride for me, and a dangerous one too. To avoid the worst of the whipping branches and the tearing thorns that Oona was bludgeoning her way through, I had to lie face down along her neck. It only took one careless glance up ahead at the wrong moment, one lapse of concentration and the damage was done. It had happened all too often in the past – I had scars all over me to prove it. I had learned time and again that [illegible] however insignificant it might seem at [illegible]

So that was why I was lying down on Oona's neck and hugging myself into it so tightly, when one morning we emerged from the jungle and into a clearing. It was safe enough now for me to dare to look up. Oona was standing still, her ears wafting gently, her trunk reaching up into the nearby trees. They were fig trees, and heavy with ripe fruit from the ground up. I sat up then and looked around me. I was amazed at what I saw – a secret horde of figs, an entire forest of fig trees, dozens of them all around the clearing.

"Must be enough here to feed a hundred elephants," I told her, leaning over and patting her neck. "And you knew it was here, didn't you? You just follow your trunk, don't you?" Out of necessity, when orange coconuts and bananas were scarce, I'd had to eat a lot of fruit in the jungle that I didn't much like, but figs were different. Figs were fantastic. Figs were my favourite. Figs were the best. I knew it was the same for Oona, that they were the delight of her life. It was obvious that we'd be staying put for a very long while, and that by the time we left the clearing, there wouldn't be a fig left.

I heard the babble of a river nearby, and caught a glimpse of it glistening through the trees, and spotted a kingfisher, bright with sudden colour, knifing through the air. The whole place was alive with hummingbirds. It was a perfect paradise. There was all the water we needed, I thought, and plenty of high trees for safe sleeping nests. "We could stay here for ever, Oona," I said. "I bet there're fish in that river too, hundreds of them." I tapped her neck then with my heel, as I always did when I wanted to be let down. But Oona wasn't responding, wasn't lowering herself for me. She wasn't eating the figs either, and that was strange. I tapped her again and again. She still wouldn't let me down.

That was when I first began to think we might not be alone, that Oona had sensed something, and wasn't sure yet what it was. I heard rustling from across the

clearing, and saw there were branches shaking, high up
in a giant fig tree. I thought maybe that our orang-utan

shapes drifting through the trees, shapes that became
orang-utans, not one, but dozens of them.

I spotted at once at least three mothers with their
babies clinging on to them, and there were several
youngsters there too, one of them hanging from a
branch by a single arm, and all of them gazing in
wonderment at Oona and me, unsure, anxious, but not
alarmed. They were more like humans than any
creature I'd ever set eyes on. Every face was individual,
different, and their eyes were filled with feeling and
with curiosity. The younger they were the wispier
their brown hair was, the more bald many of them
seemed to be. They scratched like we do, yawned like
we do.

I had seen that one orang-utan often enough in the

jungle, but only distantly, as he swung high up through the canopy. This was my first close encounter. I found myself staring back at them. The wonderment was mutual. For many long minutes it seemed none of us knew quite what to do. All any of us could do was stare. But after a while I could see that the more I stared the more agitated they were becoming. Wide-eyed with consternation, the babies were clinging ever tighter to their mothers, hiding their heads. One of them began to suckle his mother frantically, as if that might help these strange apparitions to go away. Many of them were still holding a fig to their mouths, their jaws frozen in mid-chew, not yet at ease enough to go on eating. Each was looking to the other now for comfort and reassurance.

I could see no real sign of aggression in them. A few of the younger adults were crashing around up in the treetops, but I felt that, as with the orang-utan who had shadowed us for so long through the jungle, this might be just to let us know they were there and watching, and that we had better take care not to encroach any further on their territory. I realised that any sudden movement would have been a mistake. Oona clearly sensed this too. She was moving almost in slow motion as she h

now, bunching together, mothers and infants hugging one another close.

By this time, Oona had clearly decided it was best to ignore them altogether, and just let them get used to us. She'd begun to feast on the figs from the nearest tree. The orang-utans looked on, apparently happier now, and a few of them, mostly the younger ones, were beginning to feed again, but still keeping a wary eye on us at the same time. I thought the best thing I could do was what Oona was doing, what they were doing, and eat the figs. A dozen or so of these huge ripe figs were all I could manage, and I could reach these easily enough from the ground.

When I'd finished, I climbed high into the branches of one of the fig trees where I found myself a comfortable place to sit, and a perfect vantage point from which to observe the orang-utans, who were now all much calmer, and intent on their feeding in the trees on the far side of the clearing. The three nursing mothers had settled to their feasting like the others. They ate tidily, peeling each fig and enjoying it before looking for the next one, their babies clinging on to them easily as they clambered from one branch to another, constantly on the search for better pickings.

I could see that these mothers in particular were still a little wary, still not at all sure what to make of us. Sometimes, when they had gorged themselves enough, when they were at rest in between these fig feeding frenzies, they would sit in among the leaves, and just stare at me, trying to work me out, I thought, wondering what on earth I was. There was one moment, I remember, when it felt as if all of these dozens of orang-utans, young and old alike, were gazing at me in awe and wonder. For all I knew I might have been the very first human being these creatures had ever set eyes on. One thing was for sure, I was as curious about them as they were about me. I couldn't help thinking that we didn't just look like one another, these orang-utans and me. We were like one another. We were kindred spirits

When they moved from tree to tree they had a curious way of doing it. They didn't swing through the trees as the gibbons did. They weren't lithe and loose-limbed like them. They didn't look like natural born swingers. Their technique seemed slower and more considered, more cautious. They would hang there and sway themselves from side to side until they could reach out, grab the branch they were after, and then let that branch swing them into the next tree. Every time they seemed to judge the swing just right, holding on by three hands, or two hands and a foot, and then reaching out with the fourth for the branch of the tree they wanted to climb into.

But it soon became worryingly clear to me that at least three of the younger adults weren't going to be content until they got a closer look at me. They were coming to check me out. Encouraged by their example, all the other orang-utans began to swing towards me through the branches. I noticed then, that one of the mothers, the darkest and largest of them, had the tiniest of infants clinging to her. She seemed to be leading a whole group of adults, most with babies hanging on to them. Everywhere I looked they were making their way towards me through the fig trees. I found I was being approached by orang-utans from all sides now. It was unnerving, but at no time as they came nearer did I feel really frightened. This wasn't an attack, I was sure of it – or nearly sure anyway. This was an investigation. But there were lots of them, and all their eyes were on me.

I did look around to see where Oona was, just for reassurance, but she had disappeared from sight. I knew roughly where she was though. I heard her browsing in among the fig trees, snorting and blowing and groaning from somewhere deep in the thicket. Once or twice I could make out *exactly* where she was, because I could see the branches shaking. I could hear them splitting and cracking as she dragged them down and broke them off. Like me, she had clearly decided there was no threat, that she could feed here in

moving in ever closer, until they were settled all around me in among the branches. I found myself completely surrounded. There was only one thing for it. I kept very still, sat back in the crook of the tree, crossed my legs, folded my arms, and tried to look as relaxed as I could. Now that they were this close, I noticed that they seemed to be wanting to avoid any real eye contact. They would dart looks at me, then look away. So, as I understood it, glancing was acceptable to them, but not staring. I thought it was best to do the same.

After a while the youngsters began to show off, each doing his best to out-dare and outshine the other, or so it seemed to me, as they swung through the fig tree below me, above me, and behind me. I hardly knew which way to look. They were all around me and so close now, far too close for comfort. One of them decided it would be fun to hang upside down and dangle there by one leg from a branch right above my head, so that as he swung we were almost nose to nose. Another had climbed on to the branch I was sitting on, and was shaking it vigorously, so that I had to hang on tight with both hands to prevent myself from falling off.

In the end, to my great relief, the three mothers came and sat nearby, and that seemed to calm the youngsters. They stopped their antics and sat there quietly eating figs and pretending to ignore me altogether. I did the same. I peeled a fig and tried to take absolutely no notice of them.

It was all a game, a game of patience. With orang-utans this was clearly how everyone got to know everyone. *Just do what they do*, I kept thinking, *and it'll work out fine. Hopefully.*

Oona came back shortly afterwards into the clearing. I watched her as she stood there for a few moments looking around for me. I called down to her, softly, so as not to upset the orang-utans. She didn't seem in the least surprised to find me sitting up there in the fig tree surrounded by an entire family of orang-utans. I threw her down the fig I'd been peeling. She snuffled it up off the ground, before meandering away through the trees and down towards the stream beyond. I really hadn't been at all thirsty until I saw where she was off to.

Suddenly I was longing for a drink.

I was about to climb down and follow her when I saw that one of the infant orang-utans had detached herself from her mother and was swinging herself slowly along the branch towards me. It was the smallest of them and, I presumed, the youngest too. She came and sat down so close to me, that I could have reached out and touched her. But I sensed that maybe this wasn't the right moment for me to move. I didn't want to do anything to scare her. I thought I would sit there, just be still and patient, and give my new friend the opportunity to introduce herself in her own time. Her mother – and this was the darkest of the mothers, the one who seemed to me like the leader, to carry most authority – was watching everything more than a little warily, as the young orang-utan reached up, grasped the branch above my head, swung herself up and dangled there beside me, one-handed. I looked into her eyes, and smiled at her. I found myself laughing then. I couldn't stop myself. I was hoping it wouldn't frighten her off.

What happened next took me entirely by surprise. The young orang-utan reached out towards me

...gers firmly and tugged at it. There was a strength and determination in the grip of that tiny creature that I simply could not believe. I knew there was no point in trying to pull my finger away, because I knew I wasn't going to be strong enough to break free. The youngster lifted my hand to her nose, sniffed it, touching it with her lips as she did so, before letting it fall. She looked up into my face then and touched me on the ear. I was hoping she wouldn't decide to have a grab at it, and try to yank it off.

Maybe it was partly to prevent that from happening that I spoke to her then. I didn't mean to. The words just came out. "That's my ear you've got," I said softly. I wanted to see how much I could make her understand. It seemed the natural thing to do. I thought I'd try something. I reached my hand out very slowly, and touched the infant orang-utan on her ear. "And that's your ear," I told her. I went on. "And I've got hair like you too, not shaggy and red like yours, but it's hair all the same. And you've got two hands and two feet like me. In fact, you and me, we're pretty much alike. What d'you think?"

The orang-utan was looking up at me all the time I was speaking. There was an intelligence in her face that astonished me. This was no mere animal. I couldn't help thinking to myself that this little creature was as human in spirit as I was. It made me think then, that maybe, maybe, I could be every bit as animal as she was human. It was a new thought and a troubling one.

The youngster made her way back to her mother after that, and for some time afterwards I sat there in my fig tree among the orang-utans, listening to Oona wallowing noisily in the river nearby. I imagined her whooshing herself down, drinking her fill, revelling in it, and I longed to climb down and join her. I was hot now, and listening to her in the river was only making me more thirsty than ever. I was longing for a drink, and for a swim too. I was sorely tempted to climb down and join her in the river, but I just couldn't bring myself to leave

stayed. I decided I would drink later, swim later.

With a clap of thunder so close above us that it actually shook the tree, the rains came down. The downpour was so sudden and violent that within seconds I could hardly see across to the other side of the clearing. Huddled together, hunched and bedraggled the orang-utans were sheltering as best they could under the leaves of the fig tree. But in a gusting storm like this even the huge fig leaves provided little protection. I noticed then that two of the mothers had contrived a makeshift canopy of giant leaves, holding them up over their heads, just as I had learned to do. This way both they and their babies were staying a great deal drier than the rest, and a lot drier than me too. I found I was sitting on a branch that seemed to be exposed to the worst of the storm-blast, and with hardly a leaf for shelter. Like the orang-utans, I just had to sit it out until the storm ended at last, as abruptly as it had begun, leaving the forest dripping, strangely silent and filled with mist.

Only moments later I looked down to see Oona come running through the trees into the clearing. I could see at once that she was unsettled, by the thunder perhaps, I thought, and that surprised me because she'd never shown any fear of thunder before. She was coming on a charge now, her ears flapping, her trunk lifted and trumpeting. She was warning me of something. Not since the tidal wave had I seen her this agitated.

Then I saw why. Coming out of the jungle behind her I saw three men – hunters with rifles. They were taking aim, not at her at all, and not at me, but at the orang-utans in the fig trees all around. A volley of shots rang out. Every bird and bat in the jungle lifted off in a cacophony of shrieking and screeching. Trumpeting her terror Oona stampeded across the clearing and vanished into the undergrowth. I saw the dark-haired orang-utan slump, and slip sideways from her branch. She hung there by one hand f...

...ey could go, into the tops of the fig trees. But they weren't fast enough, and nowhere was high enough. More shots rang out, and a second mother tumbled out of the tree, hitting the forest floor with a sickening thud. Stunned until now, I had come to my senses and was screaming at the hunters to stop shooting.

For just a few moments they were taken by surprise. They lowered their rifles and pointed up at me, gesticulating wildly and shouting at one another. But all too soon they began shooting again. One of the youngsters was hit in mid-swing as he tried to escape, and came crashing down through the branches above me. I had no time to get out of the way. I took a glancing blow from his body as it fell, but it was enough to make me lose my balance. I tried desperately to grab a hold, tried to save myself, but I couldn't. I remember hitting the branches as I fell through them, remember thinking it was taking a long time to hit the ground.

Then I remember nothing.

I knew I was still alive because I could hear the sound of an engine, and some music. It was several moments before I could gather my thoughts enough to realise I must be in the back of some sort of pick-up truck that was being driven at speed over rough ground, rattling violently as it went, throwing me from side to side. A radio was playing, the music loud, and close by, the whole truck vibrating with the beat of it. And there was the sound of men laughing raucously from inside the cab. They had to be the hunters I'd seen in the clearing. I could feel fingers clutching me, clawing at me. Everywhere there were warm wet bodies clinging to me and crying. I was still trying to believe this might be the worst of nightmares, and I wanted to

wake up from it. I kept trying to sit up, but I was being
rocked around so much that I couldn't stay sitting for

be.

My vision might have been blurred, but I could see
enough now to begin to make some sense of my
surroundings. I was in some kind of a wooden cage,
along with three little orang-utans, all of them
whimpering in terror, their fists gripping me tight, by
my hair, my T-shirt, my neck, my ear, wherever they
could get a hold. My feet were tied. There was no
feeling left in them. I looked up to see where I was,
where we were going. I could hardly see the sky above
me for smoke. Everywhere there was a stench of
burning. The truck was slithering and sliding in and
out of every pothole and rut it was being driven
through, jolting me violently against the bars of the
cage. From the cab, I could hear the hunters whooping

and singing. I gathered the three orang-utans close to me, my arms around them to protect them all I could.

Now it came to me, and I remembered everything. I knew well enough why they were clinging to me so tight, and why they were squealing too. Every one of them had just seen their mother killed, and I knew only too well how they must be feeling. I hugged them to me, stroking them, talking to them, trying to console them all I could. But they were inconsolable. So many questions filled my head, all of them unanswerable. Who were these hunters? Why had we been kidnapped? What were these men going to do with us? I closed my eyes, tried to calm myself, tried to think straight.

When I opened them, I found my vision was clearing itself at last, that everything was in focus again. That was when I became aware that there were eyes staring at me from the back of the truck, amber eyes, tiger's eyes. His paws were tied together, and they were lashed to a pole. He was lying there on a blood-soaked sack, his tongue tolling. This was the

same face I remembered, the same tiger that had
journeyed with us along the trail and in my dream

"He is like God here"

The evening was darkening. The pickup truck was lurching down a muddy track into what looked to me to be a small shanty town of campfires and ramshackle huts scattered all over the valley and up the hillsides. And all around as far as I could see the whole valley was stripped bare of trees, a great scar of brown earth and rock slashed through the jungle, a muddy stream running along the bottom.

Everywhere in the gloom there were swarms of men and women and children working like ants all over the valley, most of them hacking into the hillside with pickaxes, others manning sluices, some – and most of these were children – labouring uphill under heavy loads, many of them covered in mud up to their waists. I thought at once this had to be some kind of mining operation, but I had no idea at all what they could be mining for. A pall of dark pungent smoke hung over the entire valley. There were shrill voices, angry voices, and the sound of children wailing. It seemed to me that we were being taken down into a kind of hell, a place of evil, a place of sorrows.

All through that terrible journey I had tried all I could not to look at the tiger, because I found that if I did my eyes would fill with tears. But it was almost impossible not to look at him, stretched out as he was right in front of me. I knew I mustn't give in to tears, that whatever happened, the little orang-utans would be relying on me for everything now. I had to concentrate all my mind on their needs and nothing else. What they

really needed of course was to feel their mothers' arms
around them, their mothers' love, and most important

But painful or not, I had to endure it and let them
suckle on. Of course, there was little enough satisfaction
in it for them, but it was clearly of some comfort to them,
and I thought that must be better than nothing.

There were dozens of people running alongside the
pickup truck now, as it slowed and then ground at last
to a halt. Thinking this might be the last moment we
would have together, I looked long into the eyes of the
tiger. It was my way of saying goodbye, I suppose. But
from those eyes, gleaming now at me in the flickering
light of the fires, I drew all the courage and strength I
knew I would be needing, to face whatever was to come.
I promised myself then that whatever was going to
happen to us, whatever they did to us, I would cry no
tears in front of these kidnappers, these murderers. I

had a powerful feeling that the tiger was handing to me at that moment the guardianship not only of the three little orang-utans I was cradling in my arms, but of the spirit of the whole jungle.

We were already surrounded by an excitable mob, pushing and shoving to get a better look at us, at the orang-utans, at me, at the dead tiger. I was ready for them. There would be no cowering, no fear shown. I gripped the bars and glared back defiantly at every one of them. Whooping in triumph the crowd dragged the tiger out first. My eyes filled with tears despite myself, as I watched them carrying him away swinging from the pole, head hanging, limp in death. They hauled out the cage then, and we were carried away, swaying like the tiger in front of me as we were borne along through the hubbub of the crowd, the orang-utans crying in their terror, despite all I could do to comfort them.

The gathering crowd looked on in awe as the tiger passed by, but this soon turned to mocking laughter when they spotted me, and the little orang-utans, in the cage. They rattled the bars with sticks, poking and jabbing at us. They made monkey faces at us, and some of the children were laughing at us and sticking their tongues out. Everywhere there was whooping and

All this time I was trying to confront the crowd with a fixed, unflinching stare, and as I did so, I recited to myself again and again, like a mantra, the first lines of my tiger poem: "'Tyger, tyger, burning bright, in the forests of the night...'" I found the words sounded like a bugle call to me inside my head. They kept my courage from failing, they rallied my spirits.

This journey through those baying crowds was like torture for the little orang-utans, and it only ended when at last they set the cage down outside a rickety-looking wooden shack with two chimneys belching smoke at either end. The place smelled and looked like some kind of a cookhouse. I could see there were several pans left steaming on the vast stove inside, and there was a long low table covered with chopped vegetables and fruit outside, under the eaves. Everything looked as if it had been hastily abandoned in all the excitement of our arrival.

Nearby, the three hunters stood with their rifles, arms around one another, posing for photographs, the tiger stretched out on the ground in front of them. One of them – he had a red bandana around his forehead – put his foot on the tiger's head and punched the air again and again in triumph, to the evident delight of the crowd, who were cheering him wildly all the time. I remembered the red bandana now. I'd seen that man back in the clearing, and he'd been driving the pickup truck. He had the look of power about him, and seemed to me to be a ringleader. He was certainly the hero of the hour for the crowd. He hushed them easily, with a flourish of his hand, and began to make a speech, his foot still on the tiger's head.

It became clear very soon that he was telling them all the story of the hunt, and doing it dramatically, flamboyantly. I didn't understand a word of what he was saying of course, but I understood the gist of it: how they'd lain in wait by a river where the tiger came to

swim and ambushed him; how they'd shot him in the
water as he was swimming, and dragged him out. Th

one, and every time they roared their approval.

They had shot fifteen.

By this time the whole crowd was cheering and
laughing. And then, he went on, they had discovered
that one of them was not an orang-utan at all, but a
'monkey boy'. He said that in English too, and that got
the loudest laugh of all. There were more stories, more
jokes, and then the bottles came out and the drinking
began. Shortly after this, with the excitement over, they
drifted away, carrying the tiger with them, leaving us in
peace at last. The little orang-utans fell asleep, but only
fitfully, clutching me all the while.

But they didn't leave us alone for long. The mine-
workers and their families were beginning to line up for
their evening meal outside the cookhouse. As they

passed by our cage with their bowls of food, most of the children would crouch down and have a look in at us, and it wasn't just out of curiosity either. They teased us and taunted us, offering us food, and then snatching it away at the last moment. Some would put their faces to the bars of the cage and screech at me: "Monkey boy! Monkey boy!" One or two were trying out some words of English. "What are you? You monkey? You American monkey boy? You English monkey boy?" I sat there, confronting every inquisitive look, enduring every mocking grin, with the same cold gaze, all the while reciting the tiger poem silently to myself, over and over, keeping the spirit of the tiger alive inside me, keeping him strong, keeping me strong.

It was only when the last of them had gone, the cooks had left, and the cookhouse shutters were closed, that I felt I could try to get some sleep. I lay down and tried to stretch out as best I could. But the cramped cage gave me little room to move, and no comfort at all, and the little orang-utans were constantly crawling over me, always on the search for food, pestering me for it almost constantly, and there was nothing I could do to help

time they bring little orang-utans back from the jungle. Many times they bring them back. They say, 'You feed them, Kaya.' But when they very young, very small like these orang-utans, they are not so easy to feed. They do not like to take food from stranger, only from mother. But mother is dead, and they know this. They are very afraid. The hunters say to me, 'Kaya, no one buy dead orang-utan. Dead orang-utan no use to nobody, not worth a flea. If they die we beat you, Kaya.' Many times they beat me. I tell them it is not my fault, that I try my best, but sometimes little orang-utans do not take fruit from me. They are not stupid – I tell them this. I say, 'They know I am not mother. They want food only from mother. They do not want to take it from me.' And then they die. These people, these hunter men, they do not listen. They just beat me. But I think little orang-utans die from sadness inside, not because they do not eat. These ones are very sad, like the others. But I watch you. They think you are like mother. They trust you. I can see this. They will eat this food if you give it to them."

He cut the fruit and handed it through the bars to me. "Is it true?" he went on. "Are you wild monkey boy of the forest, like they say?" I took the fruit from him, but said nothing.

tearing at it, stealing from each other. I was hoping for some of it for myself, but there was no chance of that.

By the time they had finished, they were still looking for more, gnawing at the skins again and again. But it must have been enough for the moment, because they all fell asleep soon afterwards, which was more than I was able to do. I had pins and needles in so many places. I was longing to move, but I didn't dare, for fear of waking the orang-utans, who were still clinging tight to me, even in their sleep.

Kaya came back a short time later, as he had said he would, scurrying across to the cage, bent double as he ran, looking around nervously all the time. He crouched down, his face  close to the bars. "They eat it all, this fruit?" he whispered, reaching in and picking up one of the discarded skins. I nodded, but said nothing more. Kaya looked back over his shoulder again. "You must be very good mother, I think. I have water for you, boy, and I have coconut. You like coconut? My son, he like coconut very much. I have son like you, not so young as you maybe. He is back home in my village. I work here because I must feed him, I must feed all my family, my mother and father too. He is very old man now, and sick. How can they live if I do not send them money?

send me away, and then I have no work. Maybe they will kill me. These are not good people. They do bad things. The hunter men they say to me, 'Starve the monkey boy, no water, no food.' But I cannot do this." He handed me a bottle of water through the bars of the cage. I drank it without stopping, and afterwards wolfed down the coconut so fast that I almost choked on it, and then I washed it down with the last of the water.

As I handed back the bottle, I looked at him properly for the first time. He was a withered, diminutive man, his skin stretched thin over his hollow cheeks, as if life was draining out of him with every passing minute. But in his eyes he was strong, and kind too. "Thank you," I whispered.

"I will do what I can to save you, boy," Kaya said, "but I cannot do much. They watch me. Here everyone watches everyone."

"What will they do with us?" I asked him.

"They sell you maybe. Here they sell everything, the gold from under the ground, the trees they cut down, the orang-utans they capture, the tigers they shoot."

"And me?"

He shrugged. "I do not know what they will do with you, boy. Maybe they sell you too. Tomorrow Mister Anthony comes from Jakarta. He is God round here. He will decide. He decides everything round here. It is Mister Anthony who decides who works, who does not work, who lives, who dies. Everything. You sleep now, boy." He got up to go, but before he left, he crouched back down again. "You say nothing about this water I give you, boy," he whispered, "and you say nothing about the coconut, eh? If they know I have done this, they will beat me. You understand? You promise?"

"I promise," I said.

Kaya smiled at me suddenly. I noticed then that he had very few teeth. "Your babies, they are ....

she had solved all of my problems, kept me out of danger, been my protector and guide, been a mother and father to me. Now she wasn't there beside me I felt alone and abandoned, and then suddenly angry with her too. I even found myself blaming her for running off as she had, and saving herself. Why hadn't she driven the hunters away? Why hadn't she stayed to help us? And where was she now? Maybe she would still come to rescue us. Maybe she was out there now, just waiting for the right moment. She would come charging out of the jungle to save us. Yes, that was it. She would come. She had to come.

It wasn't the flies, nor the incessant chattering of the forest that would not let me sleep that night, nor the little orang-utans who lay all over me, their bodies hot and sticky. Hope and dread kept me awake, hope that Oona might somehow be coming to our rescue, and dread of what would happen to us the next day if she did not. I couldn't help wondering who this man was that Kaya had spoken of, this Mister Anthony from Jakarta who seemed to have the power of life and death over everyone in this place, including the orang-utans, including myself.

I thought of escape too, even though I knew it was quite impossible. The cage was made of wood, but strongly made and well padlocked. The more I thought about everything the more anxious I became, and the more I came to believe that unless I could find some way of escaping that night, unless Oona came for me, then the next day I might very well be sold into some kind of slavery.

In the end, to stop myself thinking about such things, to stop the panic rising inside me, I began to say the tiger poem, out loud this time – but softly, because I didn't want to wake the orang-utans. I recited it again and again. Then I decided to hum to myself all the songs I could remember one after another, all the George Formby songs we used to sing back at home, with Dad strumming away on his

football is the game," the one Dad and I would stand up and sing, along with 40,000 others, at Stamford Bridge at the end of every match. It was during one of these familiar tunes that I must have drifted off to sleep at last.

I was woken by the sound of an engine, and the splash and crunch of a car coming down the track. I propped myself up on my elbows, but only as far as I could without disturbing the still-slumbering orang-utans, and saw a huge black four-by-four with darkened windows, pulling up outside the largest of the shacks. I'd noticed it the evening before. It was the only one that had looked anything like a proper house, with proper glass windows, a veranda, and a low wooden fence all round, and there'd been a rocking chair out on the veranda right by the front door. I remembered thinking that seemed incongruously domestic in this sprawling mess of a place.

One of the workers was hurrying barefoot past the cage now to open the car door, and there were a couple of others frantically rolling out a length of matting, from the car to the steps of the veranda. Not wanting to be noticed, I shrank back in the cage, and lay down again. All I could see now were the doors of the car, its huge tyres covered with dirt, and a lot of mud-splattered legs running past me.

The man who stepped out on to the matting had highly polished brown shoes, and white trousers with immaculate creases. He walked away along the matting for a few steps. But then he stopped, turned round and came straight back towards me. He was carrying a shiny black stick. His fingers were covered in huge gold rings, at least one on every finger. Suddenly his face was there right in front of me, pale, puffed up and sweaty, with small, shining eyes, venomous eyes.

"So there you are," he began – he spoke in a kind

of drawl. "The little monkey boy they told me about.

you know what you are, monkey boy? You're a flaming nuisance, that's what you are, a flaming nuisance, a lousy spanner in the works. You know something? I don't like people who cause me problems. Best thing to do with a problem is to get rid of it, I reckon. So maybe I'll put a bullet in your head, and throw you in a hole out there somewhere in the jungle. Problem solved. But then, maybe… maybe there's a way to make a dollar or two on you first. I can always kill you later, can't I? I'll have breakfast and think about it."

He stood up. "Bring Monkey Boy up to the house. But I want the little beggar washed down good and proper first. He stinks to high heaven."

As Mister Anthony walked away through the crowd

– Kaya among them – I noticed they all lowered their eyes and bowed as he passed them by. "Now where's this lousy tiger?" he was saying. "Show me. I want to see the tiger. He'd better be a good one." He was escorted on all sides by a phalanx of bodyguards, all dressed in the same shiny black suits, every one of them carrying a rifle.

I was expecting they'd come back for me any moment, but it seemed like hours later, hours during which I tried all I could to banish the fears inside me. I tried to think of home, of Mum and Dad, of the farm, tried to see everyone and everything clear in my head, tried to imagine I was there with them, with Grandpa on his tractor, with Dad going to the football. If I was going to die, then I wanted these to be my last living thoughts. I had my eyes closed, and was trying to stay deep in my thoughts, when I heard them coming for me.

Strong arms hauled me out, holding me fast by the elbows on either side. The little orang-utans clung on tight to me wherever they could, as the men frogmarched me away. Terrified though I was, it felt good to be upright again, and moving, not cooped up.

cookhouse ready with a hosepipe, beckoning them to bring us closer. The crowd was all around us, encircling us. I wasn't that worried when they first turned on the hosepipe – it looked harmless enough. In a way I was even looking forward to it. It was going to be humiliating, being hosed down like this in public, but at least it would be cooling, refreshing. Then I saw that there was a smile on the hunter's face and I remember wondering why he was smiling.

I realised what was going to happen too late. The jet of water hit me full in the chest with terrific force, sending me reeling back across the circle. I bent myself double, cradling the orang-utans close to me, turning my back on the water, protecting them and me as best I could. But there was no escape for them *or* for me, however much I tried to turn away from it, to dodge or duck or run. There was nowhere to run to. In the end there was only one thing I could do. I dropped to my knees, and cowered there trying to use my body to shield the screeching orang-utans from the full blast of the water. This stinging torture seemed to go on for ever, pummelling every part of me, all to the raucous delight of the crowd, until at last, mercifully, there was an end to it.

I was dragged to my feet. Determined not to cry, not to betray any sign of fear, I faced down my grinning tormentor, pursing my lips, clenching my teeth to hold back the sobs that were rising inside me. Hysterical in their pain and fear, the little orang-utans squealed pitifully. I did what I could to comfort them, whispering to them all the while as I was led away. But they were beyond consoling.

Dressed in an immaculate white suit, Mr Anthony sat there in his chair, waiting for me at the top of the veranda steps, his dark glasses glinting in the sun. At his feet lay the skin of the tiger, my tiger, Oona's tiger. There were two large hunting dogs one on either side of him, eyeing me from the top of the steps. Mister Anthony waved his stick, and at once the guards let

reminded me that at least I had one friend in this place of horrors. That was something. It gave me hope. It gave me courage.

"So, my little monkey boy," Mister Anthony began, pointing his stick at me. He was making sure he was talking loud enough for everyone to hear. "You see what I did with this tiger. And I know what I'm going to do with those orang-utans. But I'm still trying to work out what I'm going to do with you. Maybe I'll let you go, give you a head start, and then set my dogs on you. How would you like that? All I have to do is say the word, and they'd hunt you down and tear you into little pieces. That would be a whole lot of fun to watch." The crowd laughed at this, and I could see he liked that. He leaned forward. "Where did you come from, eh? How d'you get here? You got a mum and a dad, or are you just a little Pommy bastard?" He chuckled at that. "You even got a name, Monkey Boy?"

I did not answer. Mister Anthony was enjoying himself. This was a performance, a power game for the benefit of the crowd. This man was toying with me, showing me and reminding everyone there who the master was, that as Kaya had told me, Mister Anthony was God here. I screwed myself up inside. I would be fearless, as fearless as a tiger. I would make my voice sound out strong. I glanced at the dead tiger, and suddenly there was no room any more for fear. The anger raging inside me drove all that away. It was my anger that was speaking out, not my courage. "I won't tell you my name. And I don't care what you do with me," I said. "You can't do me any more harm than you've done the tiger, can you? And it was you, wasn't it? Everyone here does what you tell them. The hunters killed the orang-utans, I saw them. They killed the tiger. But you're the real killer. Everyone here is afraid of you, but I'm not."

The crowd were becoming unsettled. Clearly many

of them had understood enough of the tone of what I'd
been saying to sense my defiance. Emboldened b⎯

seemed to me more and more like a snake in human
form, from his slicked-down hair, to his shining shoes,
everything was smooth and slithery. He even moved
like a snake, as he walked slowly up and down the
veranda glaring at me. I could feel his fury rising. I
knew he was about to strike. I could feel the knot of
terror growing in the pit of my stomach. I determined
to try to keep it there, not to waver, but to stand tall
and look this vile man in the eye and face him down,
no matter what he said, no matter what he did. The
little orang-utans clung to me as tight as ever. I could
feel their need, I knew how much they were relying on
me now, and that helped to keep me strong.

"Quite the little firecracker, aren't we?" I'd caught
Mister Anthony off guard, and that really bucked me

up. I could tell he was trying to laugh it off. But it was a poor attempt. Anyone could see that he was seething with fury. "You're right, Monkey Boy. Everyone here does exactly what I tell them. And it's true. I killed the tiger, killed the orang-utans, and I kidnapped those cutey looking little orang-utans you've got wrapped round you. I've killed dozens of tigers, kidnapped hundreds of little orang-utans. And I'll tell you why, sunshine, shall I?" With every word he spoke, he was becoming more worked up, more enraged.

"Money, Monkey Boy. Do you know how much they pay me in Dubai or California for a tiger skin like that? Ten thousand US dollars. That's right, ten thousand. And the Chinese, they pay a fortune for their insides, all their bits and pieces. Tiger medicine. They swear by it. The Chinese have lots of money these days, believe you me. As for those little orang-utans of yours, I'll be selling every one of those blighters back in Jakarta. Five thousand US a piece, just like that. They buy them as pets for their kids. Police officials, government officials, business people, anyone. I sell, they buy. It's what makes the world go round, sunshine." He brandished his stick. "You see that forest? You see it?"

"I see it," I said. "So what?"

England too, in Pommieland, which is where I reckon you come from by the sound of you. And I sell them back in good old Oz too – that's home territory for me. But that's not the half of it. Thing is, I got so many trees out there I don't know what to do with them, and when I don't know what to do with them, d'you know what I do? I'll tell you, Sunshine, shall I? I burn them down, make a ruddy great bonfire of the forest. And then what have I got? Land, lots of it. And what do I do with the land? I plant more trees, thousands of them, millions of them. Not the big fellows, no they take hundreds of years to grow. I want my money fast. So I grow palm trees, to make palm oil. They grow fast, fast as grass. I can't grow enough of them. The whole world is screaming for palm oil, to put in their toothpaste, their lipstick, their margarine, cooking oil, peanut butter. You like peanut butter, Monkey Boy?"

He didn't wait for an answer. He was ranting now, his eyes blazing at me. "Palm Oil. You like biscuits, Monkey Boy? Palm oil. You like chips. They cook them in palm oil. And it gets better too, Sunshine. Heard of global warming, have you? Well, I like it. Yeah, I like it a whole lot. You see, on account of all this global warming they want to save the planet, don't they? So now they're after palm oil to run their cars, instead of petrol and diesel. All I do, Monkey Boy, is provide what the world wants. I'm just saving the planet. Oh yeah, and I'm saving the people too. I pay them. I feed them. I house them. They come from poor villages where there's no work. They cut down the trees for me, burn the forests, plant the palm trees. They look for gold for me too, dig it out, and I sell it, like I sell everything else. That's why I'm just about the richest man in Jakarta. I've got four houses, two Ferraris, and a garden bigger than a flaming football pitch. Not bad, eh? And you know what money is, Monkey Boy? I'll tell you. Money is power."

Now he was shaking his stick at me, a crazed look on his face, and screaming at me. "I could have you

fire, they'd do it. If I—" Suddenly he paused. "Now there's a thought, Monkey Boy," he said.

He was coming down the veranda steps now. Then he was right up close to me, calmer now, but still breathless from all his ranting. He was so close that I could see the spittle on his lips. "Talking of jumping through hoops of fire, I don't reckon I need to kill you after all, Monkey Boy. Aren't you the lucky one? No, I've suddenly had a much better idea, and the best kind of idea too, a moneymaking idea. I'll sell you, and I've thought of just the right place for you. I know somewhere they'd pay good money for a monkey boy like you, no questions asked. There are circuses all over India where you could be quite the little star – I've sold orang-utans to them before. I can see it now, up there in lights. 'Monkey Boy, the only all singing, all dancing monkey boy in the whole wide world!' Can you do a few tricks, cartwheels, handstands? Can you jump through hoops of fire? No? Well, can you dance? Can you sing? Go on, give us a song, sunshine; do a little dance for us."

I said nothing. Mister Anthony leaned forward and whispered in my ear. "You will dance, Monkey Boy, you will sing, or I will have those cutey little orang-utans killed right now, right in front of your eyes. Don't think I won't. There's plenty more where they come from, I promise you." He stepped back. "You hear me, Monkey Boy? Dance!"

I knew without a shadow of doubt that this man meant every word he said, that I had to do what he said. I had no choice. So I closed my eyes and began to dance, shuffling awkwardly at first from foot to foot.

"Dance, you little bastard, dance!" he yelled. I tried to let my body go looser, so that I was swaying as well as shuffling, humming all the while now to the little orang-utans, humming to help me dance. "That's better, Monkey Boy, that's better. Give us a little turn."

Mister Anthony was laughing at me now, and when moments later he began to clap, the whole crowd joined

I sang the first song that came into my head, sang it out as loud as I could, like I always did with Dad. I sang it with my eyes open, glaring up at him, looking him full in the face, unflinching. It turned out to be just the right song to have chosen, because it kept me brave, and because I could sing it with real passion. And it was a song that transported me at once to another place, another time, so that I could become another person altogether, so that I could make believe I was not there, that it was not me that this was happening to.

"*Blue is the colour, Football is the game,*
We're all together, and winning is our aim..."

Soon the whole crowd had fallen quiet. I could sense every one of them listening. This seemed to unnerve Mister Anthony. He had suddenly had enough. He waved his stick to silence me. "So," he said, his smile thin-lipped and triumphant, "so now you see how it is, Monkey Boy. You're just the same as them. They do what I say. You do what I say. You all jump through my hoops. It wasn't so bad, was it? I think you'll do very well in that circus in India. More to the point, you'll fetch me a mighty good price too." Then he turned on his heel and walked back up the steps, wiping his feet on the tiger skin on the veranda.

If he hadn't done that, and if I hadn't been so angered by it, I don't think I would ever have had the nerve to do it. I didn't think about it. I just began reciting the tiger poem at the top of my voice, very slowly, very deliberately, so that everyone there in the crowd could hear every word, so that those who could understand the words would understand, and those who couldn't would understand their meaning and my meaning from the tone of my voice.

I was aiming every word at Mister Anthony's back, and every word was an arrow of defiance. I had nothing

on Mister Anthony never wavering, until the last verse, when I looked away, because I felt the tears coming into my eyes then, and I did not want him to see them. I had eyes now only for the tiger. I spoke the last lines to him, for him, and for him alone.

> " 'Tyger, Tyger burning bright
> In the forests of the night.
> What immortal hand or eye
> Dare frame thy fearful symmetry?' "

When I had finished, the crowd stayed hushed. I saw that same flicker of uncertainty on Mister Anthony's face. It was a victory of sorts – for me, for the little orang-utans, for the tiger. I knew, after all that had happened, and with all that was going to happen to us, that it was only a little victory, but it meant a great deal to me all the same. It meant I had not surrendered, that I could at least hold my head high as I was led away through the crowd, back to our cage behind the cookhouse.

I sat there all day long in the cage with the orang-utans, trying to comfort them as best I could. There were always dozens of curious miners and their families around the cage, pushing and shoving to get a better look at us. And although most of them came only to mock, there were a few families, often those with small children, who just squatted there gazing at us, fascinated, it seemed, as much by me as by the orang-utans.

When they dared – and they dared more when I smiled at them, I discovered – some of the smaller children in particular would reach in and touch my hair, and would even let the little orang-utans hold on to their fingers. They would giggle then, and I loved to hear that. There was a curiosity and a gentleness in their eyes that gave me new heart, and as the day wore kept reminding me just how hungry I was. The orang-utans could smell it too, which was a relief to me, because after a while they stopped pestering me for food, and hung on to the bars, looking longingly across to the cookhouse. One or two of the children did try to feed them scraps through the bars of the cage, but the foremen soon shouted at them and shooed them away.

All this time Kaya never once even glanced in our direction, and I began to wonder if he had forgotten about us altogether. As it turned out, he did come again, but it wasn't until darkness fell that evening. The familiar night chorus from the jungle started up, and that was a great comfort to me, to know it was so close. But it was soon drowned out by the sound of music pulsating from Mister Anthony's house, and there was raucous laughter and wild whooping going on inside. I was sitting there thinking about how it would be for me in the circus in India, whether there'd be elephants. I was hoping there would be, then I got to thinking about Oona again, longing for her to come for us, praying she would. And that's when I saw Kaya coming running through the darkness towards us, from the now deserted cookhouse. He had a basket with

enough, and was quickly reduced to picking up their scraps, so I was over the moon when Kaya took a small bowl from his basket and handed it to me through the bars. It was rice! I put my back to the orang-utans and shovelled it into my mouth before they even noticed I had it. Luckily for me they were still intensely occupied eating their fruit. Kaya had brought us bottles of water too, enough for all of us. I helped each one of them drink it down, then I drank the rest myself, until there wasn't a drop left. Kaya waited until I had finished drinking before he said anything.

"I like very much this poem you spoke," he whispered. "I know it also. I learn it in my mission school long time ago, when I was a boy like you. Fine poem. It stay in my head for ever, I think." He looked

 about him nervously, then leaned forward. "Listen, I have bad news for you. I serve the food in the house for Mister Anthony and the hunters. They have big party in there. They celebrate killing of the tiger. I hear them talking. They are telling him you must be killed, because you have seen their faces. You know who they are. You could tell the police. It is against the law to kill tiger, to take orang-utan. If they are caught they go to prison for long long time. They know this. So they tell Mister Anthony, "Do not sell him to the circus. You must kill this monkey boy." I am very much afraid Mister Anthony will do this. You know his face too. You know too much. You must leave this place. You must escape."

"But how?" I asked him. "Look at that padlock. There's no way of getting it open without a key. Have you got the key?"

Kaya shook his head. "No," he said. "But I have been thinking, and maybe we do not need a key after all. What is it you say in English? There is more than one way to skin a rabbit. Listen to them. They are busy with their drinking. If we are lucky, if we are careful,

track, cross over the other side, and you are there. You are wild boy. I think you know very well how to hide in the jungle. But when you go you must go fast, and you must not stop. Mister Anthony's dogs. When he finds you have escaped, he will send them after you."

"Won't they know it was you that helped me?"

"I do not think so. This Mister Anthony, I have been cook for him in his house since he was a little boy. When he was young he was not so bad, you know; maybe a little greedy, like many of us I think. But the greed in him, it grew, and became the devil inside him. And now he is a bad man, a wicked man. He does not trust me, he does not trust anyone, but he will think I am too frightened to do this thing. And before I hear you speak your poem today, he was right to believe this. All my life, until now, I was frightened, like everyone here. Then I listen to the tiger poem. I remember it. I see the skin of tiger lying on the veranda. I see you and the orang-utans shut in this cage. I see men and women and little children working like slaves all around me, and I am not frightened any more."

He got up to go. "I come back very soon. I bring you coconut too. I go now."

Kaya was as good as his word. Within minutes I saw him emerging from the cookhouse. But almost at the same moment the door of Mister Anthony's house opened suddenly, and a shaft of light spilled out into the darkness. Two men came staggering down the steps, one with a rifle over his shoulder, both of them loud with drink. Kaya froze where he was, and for a moment I thought they might not see him. But they did. One of them called him over, and Kaya turned, walking towards them slowly, reluctantly. When they shouted at him he broke into a limping run. I could see that he had the coconut in his hand, that the other hand he held behind his back, and I wasn't sure why, until I saw the blades of the kitchen knives glinting

the hosepipe one, the one with the red bandana, the one I feared most.

"Monkey Boy, Monkey Boy," he called out in a mocking singsong voice. "This time I shoot you proper, Monkey Boy." He was aiming the barrel of his rifle right at my head. I hugged the orang-utans close to me, turned my head away, closed my eyes, and waited for it to happen. I filled my whole mind with thoughts of Dad and Mum and Grandpa and Grandma and Oona, and held them there, so that they would be with me right to the very end. For long long moments nothing happened. Then I heard howls of laughter. I opened my eyes, to see the two of them walking away into the darkness, arms round each other's shoulders, hysterical with drunken giggles. Kaya waited until they were well and truly gone, before he ran over to the cage.

"We must work quickly," Kaya whispered. "No talk. No noise."

He handed me a knife. We chose a bar each, and set to work at once. The bars were thick, the wood hard, and each of them seemed to take for ever to saw through. But it wasn't the time it was taking that worried me so much. It was the noise we were making as we sawed. It sounded loud, loud and rasping, too loud to be a frog, too rasping to be any part of the jungle chorus. I was sure that sooner or later someone must hear it. We couldn't do anything about the noise, but I could do it quicker. I got up on to my knees, so that I could saw harder, work faster. It wasn't at all easy, because any movement inside the cage was so restricted, and because the orang-utans would keep clinging to my arms and my shoulders. From time to time I was forced to stop sawing altogether so I could detach them and resettle them elsewhere.

Kaya had told me the knives would be sharp, and they were too, and with serrated blades . After several might already be on my trail that drove me on to greater and greater efforts, when my whole body was screaming at me to stop for a rest. I knew I mustn't stop. The clinging orang-utans were as much a part of me now as my own arms and legs, a constant reminder that if the dogs caught up with us, it wouldn't only be me they would tear to bits.

I walked on from darkness into dawn, and through all the next day, stopping only for a few brief minutes to let the orang-utans drink from a river, and to drink myself. But I soon realised that even this short stop had been a mistake. When I tried to go on again afterwards my legs had stiffened, my feet were on fire with pain, and far from being reinvigorated, all my strength seemed to have drained away. I knew I could not go on much longer. I wanted to believe that I must have put enough distance between ourselves and Mister Anthony's mining camp by now, that any pursuing dogs and hunters could never catch us up.

I had to tell myself this again and again, to reassure myself it was true, before at last I was convinced it was safe to stop. I found the right kind of tree, climbed

high into its branches, where we made ourselves a
sleeping nest of branches and leaves. The rain came

Other One

was woken by the orang-utans stirring around me in the nest, then climbing all over me. I pushed them off. I was too sleepy to cope with them. They gave up on me after a while and two of them began to wander off, climbing in among the branches nearby. Still half asleep, I let them go where they wanted. I knew they'd come back if they needed me.

One of them was trying to drink some rainwater from a hollow in a tree, another was chewing on a young leaf bud. But the smallest of them stayed closer to me – she always did – never letting go of me, even as she gnawed one-handed on a piece of bark. All of them were alert to everything that was going on around them, always looking, listening, scenting. If there was any danger, they would very soon let me know. I was still too exhausted to care much about anything. I drifted off to sleep again, but slept only fitfully.

I remember I was having one of those strange, deeply disturbing dreams, where you somehow know that you're only dreaming, but all the same it's terrifyingly real. All I wanted to do was to wake up, but I couldn't. I could hear the baying of hunting hounds. Oona was standing there at the edge of the clearing, the fig trees all around. Everywhere the ground was littered with the bodies of dead and dying orang-utans. Then out of the forest came the hunting dogs. Mister Anthony was there with them, with his hunters, and the dogs were baying for blood. Oona was trumpeting, tossing her trunk at them, as the dogs leaped at her. All the trumpeting and baying sounded loud in my head, so loud that it woke me at last.

somewhere below me in the forest, not that far away, and closer all the time. I could hear men's voices now. I saw them then – hunters with dogs yelping and straining on their leashes, some with machetes, some with rifles. They were coming our way. I counted two dogs and half a dozen men with rifles, one with a red bandana. But none of them looked like Mister Anthony.

They were right underneath us now. There was nothing else to do but to lie low in the sleeping nest, hold on tight to the orang-utans, and hope and pray they wouldn't move or whimper, that the hunters wouldn't look up and see us. I buried my face in their hair, willing them to be still, not to make a sound. I could hear the dogs yapping and yowling, as they rummaged through the leaves at the bottom of the tree, searching for the scent we must have left there. I was sure they must find it sooner or later, and that it would lead them directly to us. I closed my eyes.

I didn't breathe.

For several heart-stopping moments I lay there listening to them snuffling about, pinning all my hopes now on the rain that had fallen the night before, that it might have washed away the scent of us. Then I heard them moving away. I could breathe again. I dared to look down, and saw that one of the dogs was still reluctant to go. He was agitated, excited. I was sure he'd found something, that he was on to us. But the hunter in the red bandana yelled at him, jerking him on his lead, dragging him away. They were gone.

For a long time afterwards I could still hear them moving further and further away into the forest, slashing and beating their way through it, shouting at one another as they went. With every moment their voices became more distant. It seemed an age before the chatter and screech of the jungle quietened down around us. Only then could I really be sure they were gone.

Even so, I knew I had to stay where I was with the orang-utans, that the hunters and the dogs might not be

we would be out of harm's way. How I would do it, or whether I could do it, I had no idea. But I knew there was nothing else for it. I had to try.

Once I started looking, I soon discovered that we didn't need to go down on to the forest floor anyway, that there was enough food up here to live on, all the fruit we would need, if only I could get to it. A few trees away there were orange coconuts and some bananas too. I spotted the same kind of prickly fruit that Kaya had given us back in the cage. I'd seen that growing high up in a nearby tree. I thought there was a good chance I could reach most of the fruit I could see. It would be difficult and dangerous, but it had to be done. I would have to leap from one tree into another.

I knew I was taking my life in my hands, but I had no

choice. There was plenty of fruit there, all we needed for days. I had to try. I left two of the orang-utans in the nest – the little one wouldn't be left – and made my bid for the fruit, climbing and swinging through the branches, never once looking down. I made it, I made it there and back, again and again. We would have all the fruit we needed, for a while at least.

We were all right for drink too. There was milk from the orange coconuts. It took a while to stab through the outer skin with a pointed stick to get at the milk, but it was worth the effort. I had to fight the little orang-utans off to have my share. They loved it as much as I did.

But we had to make do with water mostly. The orang-utans always seemed to find enough, from the giant leaves that were so often filled and refilled with rainwater, and sometimes from the hollows of trees where it always seemed to be plentiful. We might have had to share the water with frogs and beetles and all sorts, and it might

not have tasted that wonderful, but it kept us going, kept us alive. Above all we were safe up here. It was all that mattered.

The more I thought about it, the more I felt sure it was best to stay where we were, that there was no point

ever in this jungle. I could even end up back near Mister Anthony's mining camp, the last place in the world I ever wanted to see again. No, staying put was best, staying put was safest.

So for many days and nights I tried to live as orang-utans and gibbons did, high in the trees, feeding off them, living off them, hiding in them, sleeping in them. I kept reminding myself of a lesson Oona had once taught me, that I had to set aside all hopes, all expectations, and to live only for today, because it was the only way to survive. But that was a great deal easier said than done.

My constant hope was that Oona might somehow find me. I kept the hope alive in my mind every day, every night. Often I'd find myself lying there in our sleeping nest telling the little orang-utans all about Oona, about how she'd saved me from the *tsunami*, about how one day she would come and find us in the jungle. But it was a hope that was fast fading with every passing day. I went on telling them about her, promising them she would come, because deep down I needed to keep believing it might be possible, that however unlikely it might be, a reunion with Oona could happen. They seemed to love gazing up into my face as I was telling my stories about her, reaching out to touch my face with their fingers, and sometimes with their lips too. Kissing, I discovered, was not just for human beings. And nor was storytelling.

I remember I was lying there once in the sleeping nest, telling them all about the farm in Devon, about Grandpa and the tractor, when I heard a sudden hooting from high above us in the canopy. It sounded like an owl. At once an image came into my head – of Mum sitting on my bed when I was little, and telling me a story about an owl who was afraid of the dark. And here I was, like an owl up in a tree, telling a story, just as she had. I cried for her that night, and for Dad, for the first time in a long while.

Living so closely together up in the trees, I was getting to know the three little orang-utans as individuals

I suppose that was why I decided in the end to call the orang-utans Bart, Tonk and Charlie. They were all very distinctive characters, so I twinned them up with whichever friend back home seemed to suit them best. The biggest of them, the strongest, and certainly the most pushy, and probably the eldest, I called Tonk. He had less hair than the others, just like Tonk back home, and like that Tonk too, he could be a bit boisterous and rough. But Tonk could sulk when things didn't quite turn out the way he wanted. Bart on the other hand, was a gentler soul altogether, always in Tonk's shadow, but a lot cleverer than him. He was the one who could always seem to work out how to find the leaves with the most water in them, when none of the others could, or how to use sticks best when he was probing for ants.

Ants, I was discovering, were a special orang-utan favourite. Tonk's hair was lighter in colour, and he had the deepest set, darkest, most thoughtful eyes.

So the littlest of the three I had to call Charlie. I wasn't sure, but I'd always thought Charlie had to be the one that had belonged to the mother orang-utan I remembered from the day of the slaughter in the fig trees, the dark-haired one that the other mothers had all looked to as a leader, the one I'd seen falling out of the fig tree, that I watched hitting the ground, still clutching her baby. Charlie was definitely more of a loner, quickly becoming more adventurous than the other two, and increasingly independent of them, though still very attached to me, literally. She was also a girl – there's a way of telling these things – unlike the Charlie at school. It made me smile every time I thought how furious Charlie would have been if he knew he'd been turned into a girl. But then of course Charlie shouldn't really have been that upset, because Charlie was a name that could be used both ways, so to speak. So it was fair enough, I reckoned, to call Charlie, Charlie.

Charlie might have been the most adventurous, but she was the most sensitive too, the most easily

to kiss my nose in particular, I don't know why.

She had thin wispy hair that stood up on the top of her head, so that she looked in a permanent state of shock. Her eyes looked like upside-down commas facing one other. There was something comical about her, but like a clown, always a sense of sadness too, even when she was fooling around and showing off. She was the best athlete of them all, which was just as well, because Tonk and Bart could gang up on her sometimes. But she always had the speed and the agility to swing away and get herself out of trouble. The boys could get jealous of her, and were inclined to give her a bit of a hard time if I ever gave her too much attention. So I did all I could to share my affection out as evenly as possible.

In the end I found that I couldn't stay up there in the sleeping nest where we'd made our home for as long as I'd hoped. The trouble was that the little orang-utans frequently fouled the nest, and it soon began to smell, and that brought the flies. Besides, we were fast running out of accessible fruit where we were. I was having to climb further and further from the nest to find it, taking greater risks all the time. If I'd had the strength and skill I would have been able to move through the trees like an adult orang-utan. I'd seen, on that terrible day in among the fig trees, how they'd reach out, grab a branch, bend it, then let the spring of the branch swing them across into the next tree where there was more fruit.

But I couldn't do that.

I could climb well enough by now, and fearlessly too. I was balancing and leaping more confidently all the time, but I knew I'd never be able to swing through the jungle like an orang-utan. I didn't have the strength, in my arms and shoulders, nor in my fingers. I didn't have the flexibility.

I realised that sooner rather than later I was going to

have to risk it. I would have to climb back down to the forest floor, and go on a search to discover another

foliage around to hide us from any prying eyes on the ground. But I was still reluctant to make the move, to take the risk.

As it turned out it was something else altogether that finally persuaded me that we had to move on. One afternoon in the heat of the day, as we all lay resting in the sleeping nest, I heard the sound of rustling from somewhere high above us. I thought little of it, but the more it went on, the more the little orang-utans became alarmed. They kept squeaking, and darting frantic looks upwards. To begin with I couldn't see what it was they were getting so agitated about.

Then I saw it, the dark shape of a large orang-utan, moving stealthily through the canopy. He was sitting there studying us now, scratching his neck, yawning, his eyes never leaving us. It was obvious he had no intention of going away. He'd come to stay. I didn't have the impression he was annoyed with us, and certainly not angry. He wasn't displaying or shaking the branches at us, but he wouldn't leave us alone, and the little orang-utans were working themselves up into a frenzy of anxiety. It occurred to me after a while that the orang-utan up there was telling us in his own way that this was his tree, that we should move on, and that if we didn't, then he might turn nasty. I realised by now that the only way I could calm the little orang-utans down was to move, and move now. But even after I'd made up my mind, I spent just a few moments sitting in the nest, listening out for any telltale alarm calls from the jungle, before finally deciding it was safe to climb down.

Once back down on the forest floor, all three of the orang-utans clung to me more tightly than ever, terrified, I think, that the orang-utan might be following us. I didn't see him or hear him again, and in fact I soon forgot about him altogether. But they didn't. I talked to them softly, hummed my songs to them – I'd found they liked the Chelsea song best –

and the further we walked the more I could feel them relaxing. I was becoming less worried myself too

into my head, the same idea I'd had a long time ago when I'd been with Oona: that if I followed a stream, then it must lead me to a river, and I could follow any river to the sea. And maybe, maybe, there was just a chance that Mum might be there, that she might have survived, might still be alive. I thought I had put all that out of my head a long time ago, but I found the hope was still there. It was possible. She could be looking for me right now. I couldn't stay in this jungle and hide for ever, hoping that Oona would come and find us. I had to get out, I had to try to find Mum. I would stick close to the stream and go wherever it led me. I would find a tree where we could lie up each night, feed as we went, just keep going.

It was then, as we were walking along the banks of

the stream, that I noticed the little orang-utans seemed rather nervous of the water. To begin with, they wouldn't go anywhere near it. But they didn't much like being left on the bank either. The more they saw me enjoying it though, drinking it, swimming in it, washing in it, the closer they dared to come to the water's edge. Charlie was the first to dip her finger in, then to try to drink from it. Then all three of them were doing it, nervously still, but doing it all the same. But however much I tried to encourage them and tempt them in, they drew the line at following me into the water to swim.

As we travelled on day after day, I never ceased to be surprised at how quick they were to imitate me, how quick to learn, even when it came to walking. Although they would generally go about on all fours when they were walking or running, they would sometimes now get up on two legs, especially if they were close to me. Charlie in particular seemed to prefer it, and would often walk upright alongside me, holding my hand.

I had only to throw a stick, and one of them would pick up another stick and do the same, and then like as not they would all join in. Whatever I did they liked to be doing too, except swimming. When the time came

finding their own way of doing whatever I was doing. Branches I could not hope to bend, they managed with ease, and they seemed to know instinctively what branch was needed and where. There was such power in their arms and shoulders, and in their fingers too.

The longer we were together on our journey down the stream, the more I came to wonder at just how similar we were. The orang-utans seemed to me to be capable of so many of our emotions and feelings: affection, jealousy, fear, pain, anger, sympathy, empathy, joy and sorrow. I saw that they learned just as we learn, by example, and by trial and error. And like small children they loved the fun of play. It was when we all four played together, hiding games, ambushing, chasing, wrestling with one another, that I became aware of just how much they trusted me now, how much they saw me as one of them. As far as they were concerned I was their mother. As far as I was concerned, they were my children.

But what I truly loved about these creatures was how *un*human they were. They seemed quite incapable of any kind of calculated violence or cruelty, such as I had witnessed in Mister Anthony's camp. These were peaceful creatures, generous-hearted. Yes, I had known people like them – Kaya for one, my own family, and my friends back home too. But the more I thought about it, and I thought about it a lot, the more I was coming to believe that deliberate cruelty was to be found only in humankind, men like Mister Anthony who killed for greed and pleasure, men who destroyed the world about them.

Whenever we'd found the right tree and settled in for the night, we would very soon discover we had inquisitive visitors from all around the forest. The first to come were usually the gibbons, swooping and swinging down through the canopy above to check us out. They would stay for a while, howling and hooting at us, showing off their astounding athletic versatility.

When they'd finished a performance, they would sit
around for a while watching us, but sooner or later they

by whole families of long-tailed lemurs. And red-
bottomed monkeys with flashing eyes would approach

us through the trees and watch us, but they never came too close. All of these visitors were nervous enough to keep their distance. They were just curious. The young orang-utans showed little interest in them. They kept their eye on them, but they didn't seem at all fearful.

It was only when that same orang-utan appeared one morning in the canopy above our sleeping nest, rummaging around as if he meant us to notice him, that they became at all alarmed.

The moment I saw him, I had no doubt it was the same orang-utan who had bothered us before, and the uncomfortable truth was that if it was him, then like as not, he was following us. And only then, as this realisation sank in, did it occur to me that this might even be the same orang-utan who had shadowed Oona and me through the jungle all that time ago. He didn't scare me, but as the days passed and he was still up there, still following us, it did unsettle me.

The little orang-utans, on the other hand, seemed to get used to having him around, and ignored him almost completely. He was so often with us – more often than not now – that we all began to think of him as a travelling

One'. I'd call up to him sometimes, and wave. "Morning Other One," I'd say. I'd only get a long dark look in reply, of course. He was good at long dark looks. Then after several days with us, he just wasn't there any more. I missed him. I think the little orang-utans did too.

I was beginning to find the long days trekking along the stream more than a little disheartening. Other streams did join it, and it joined other streams, but it never became the river I was looking for, the one that would take me to the sea, and back to Mum. And that was another thing I wasn't coping with well at all. In my mind's eye I kept seeing that great green wave coming in, and the devastation it brought with it, and I realised more and more that I was hoping for the impossible. I would follow the stream, I would try to get to the sea,

I would keep going, but I knew in my heart of hearts that it was just kidding myself in my desperation to believe that Mum could have survived. I tried, as I'd tried before, to put that hope out of my mind once and for all. I had to try to concentrate all my energies on the little orang-utans, on finding us food, on keeping safe, keeping strong.

Instead, I turned to the only real hope I had left – Oona. During the day I was always too busy looking after the little orang-utans to think of her that much. But every night now as I lay listening to the forest around me, I'd make a point of closing my eyes and thinking of her. I'd wonder where she was and what might have become of her, how long it would be till I saw her again.

I had no idea how she was ever going to be able to find me in the immensity of this jungle. But I told myself she would, that she was out there somewhere, that she was alive. We were living under the same stars, the same moon, listening to the same din of the jungle. Every night I tried to fill my heart with fresh hope, hope that she was still looking for me, that one way or another our paths would cross. Another reason then to follow the stream, I thought. She needed water, she loved water. If

I hoped hard enough, I thought, then it might happen, it might. Keep believing – every night, it was the last

the jungle, I thought that I must be imagining it, still in my dreams. Only when I heard it again some time later – more fully awake by now – did I begin to dare to hope that it hadn't been a dream, that my ears might not be deceiving me. Charlie was sitting on my shoulders, grooming me, delving into my hair with her fingers, an established morning ritual by now. She stopped her grooming. She had heard it too. She climbed at once on to my lap, her eyes wide with alarm. Tonk and Bart were already gone from the nest, playing somewhere nearby, but they came scurrying back, and sat there with Charlie, all of them clutching me. Still not allowing myself to quite believe it, I waited until I heard it again. When it came this time, it was louder, closer, more urgent.

It was real!

I wasn't imagining it. The trumpeting echoed through the forest. Gibbons and lemurs scattered screeching high into the treetops. Clouds of birds and bats rose into the air, filling the forest with their thunderous din.

The little orang-utans were becoming frantic by this time, as the trumpeting sounded out again, and again, and again. She was calling me, I was sure of it. It had to be her! It had to be Oona! But now it seemed to me as if the trumpeting was coming from further away. She was moving away from me. I had to go after her. I had to let her know I was there, that I was still alive. I was yelling out now at the top of my voice, terrified that the moment might have passed, that it was too late, that my last chance of rescue was gone for ever.

I did not hesitate any more. I was on my feet in the sleeping nest. With the little orang-utans clinging on where they could, I began the long climb down, talking to them all the way, reassuring them as best I could. "We've got to find her," I told them. "She won't hurt you, I promise. Just hang on." And hang on they did, like limpets, their sharp little nails digging into me, as I shinned down the tree to the forest floor. Leaving the stream behind us, I set off through the jungle as fast as my legs could carry me, in the direction of Oona's last

and praying she might have found the same track and be following it too. Suddenly it occurred to me that the hunters and their dogs followed tracks, maybe this track, that I could just as easily be walking towards them, as towards Oona – or away from her come to that. But even as I was thinking all this, I dismissed it as unlikely. I hadn't heard or seen anything of the hunters in a long time now. They must surely have given up the chase by now and gone back to Mister Anthony's mine. There was a risk, though, and I knew it. But I had no choice. If I was to find Oona, I had to take the risk. I had to go on looking for her, go on calling for her. So, time and again I stopped, cupped my hands to my mouth, and shouted out as loud as I could, "Oona! Oona! Oona!"

It was loud enough to upset a few starlings and doves and to send them fluttering skywards, and to flush a pair of squawking peacocks out of the undergrowth. But I could tell that my voice was not carrying, not far enough anyway. The jungle was simply soaking it up, stifling the echoes. Even so, I never gave up trying. Every time I called her, I'd stand there and listen, waiting for a response, listening for it, longing for it. But none came.

The little orang-utans clearly hated it whenever I stopped to shout for her. They kept hiding their heads against me, clinging to me and to one another. I think they must have thought I was angry with them. I stroked them, put my arms round them and hugged them. "It's all right," I told them. "It's all right. Only once more, I promise you. I'll call her just once more."

Ahead of us now I saw there was a great mound of grey rock rearing up through the trees from the jungle floor, a miniature mountain shaped a bit like a giant ant hill. That was the place to do it, I thought. If I could manage to climb to the top of it, then maybe my voice might carry further. I knew it was going to be a difficult climb. And it was too. Handholds and footholds were difficult to find, the rock face wet and treacherous, and all the time Charlie was hanging tight round my neck

no longer. There was no answer except for the rasping of some nearby frogs that I must have disturbed. Once they'd begun, others answered until the whole jungle was loud with frogs.

I sat down on the rock in deep despair. I did not doubt for one moment that it had been Oona out there, that she had been searching for me, calling for me, and that she had now wandered away out of earshot. We had been so near to one another, yet so far. I put my head in my hands and cried. Almost at once little fingers were prising away my fingers. Charlie was looking up at me, reaching out and touching my mouth. Her eyes were telling me that she didn't like to see me sad, that I had her, that I wasn't alone.

"I'll be fine, Charlie," I said, wiping my tears away

with the back of my hand, and I knew I had to be too, that I mustn't give in to despair. I had to be fine, I would make myself be fine. "You've got to chill, Will." I said it out loud. "That's what Dad used to say, Charlie. You've got to chill, Will. Where there's a Will there's a way – that was another one of his jokes. He was full of jokes, my dad." But no words, not even those could lift my spirits. I closed my eyes to stop the tears coming again, and they would have come too, had Charlie not insisted on opening my eyelids too. I was thinking that Charlie, just like Oona, spoke with her eyes. She was telling me to cheer up. So I did. I smiled back at her, and I could see that made her happy again.

She heard it before I did, and looked up. So did Tonk and Bart. They weren't alarmed, but they were excited, surprised. Then I saw him too, high above us, swinging through the branches. It was Other One. He'd come back. I was so pleased to see him. But there was something strange going on, something I couldn't understand at all. I thought I could hear him breathing. But that wasn't possible, because he was far away, thirty, maybe forty feet above us. Yet I was definitely hearing the sound of breathing, heavy breathing.

In fact it wasn't just breathing, it was heaving, it was

for me. And walking along on all fours just behind her was another dark-haired orang-utan, a female. Like Oona, she had stopped now, and was gazing up at me.

"What kept you, Oona?" I said. And then the tears did come.

Burning bright

nce down off the rock, I set the three little orang-utans down on the ground. With Oona there towering over them, they were reluctant to leave me at first, but then Charlie seemed to recognise the dark-haired orang-utan as one of her own. She needed no encouragement after that. Giving a wide berth to Oona, she scampered over to what must have seemed to her at long last to be a

proper-looking mother. Tonk and Bart followed, and soon the mother orang-utan was being besieged by all three. She looked a little overwhelmed, as they clambered all over her, but perfectly happy. I noticed though that it was with Charlie that she was at her most attentive, most affectionate.

Oona's trunk was the only part of her I could hug – I'd done it often enough before. I waited for the deep rumble of contentment that I remembered so well, and sure enough it came, vibrating all through her, and all through me too. It was so good to feel that wrinkled roughness again, to trace once again the patterns of the pinkish markings in her skin, to look up into her all-seeing eyes, to be wafted again by her great ears. She was still dusty from some recent mud bath, and a bit smelly too, but it was an old familiar smell, that I found as reassuring as the rest of her.

She was turning then, kneeling for me, her trunk curling around and lifting me up on to her neck. I was back where I loved to be, where I belonged. I caught a glimpse of Other One too, sitting high up above us in among the leaves, looking down on us all, satisfaction written all over his face, as if he had engineered this whole thing, had somehow brought us all together.

Charlie, Bart, Tonk, I told you Oona would come looking for us. I knew she'd find us. I knew it." But the little orang-utans were far too busy with their new-found mother, to be listening to me at all. They were all over her and all over each other too, squealing with excitement, jockeying for the best place to get the most attention. She was sharing it out as well as she could, but the longer I watched the more it became clear to me that little Charlie might well be her own baby, that she was without any question her favoured one. She was the only one she was allowing to try to suckle, her little fists clenched tight in her mother's straggly brown hair.

Bart and Tonk were not rejected as such, not pushed away. They were allowed to cling on, but not to interfere with Charlie. As I looked on, I felt overwhelmed by a huge sense of relief. Not only was I safely back with Oona, but the three little orang-utans I had looked after all this time had survived their ordeal, and were at last reunited with one of their own kind.

I noticed then for the first time that there was a livid red scar across the mother orang-utan's forehead, and that she often held her left arm up across her chest, supporting it if she could with her other hand, as if she was nursing a damaged shoulder. I was sure of it then. This had to be the mother I'd seen falling out of the fig tree that day, the one that had been lying there, dead as I had thought, with her baby still clutching her. And Charlie was that baby.

A bullet must have grazed the mother's forehead. She'd fallen out of the fig tree, and had lain there unconscious on the ground, while the hunters grabbed Charlie and carried her off. I knew well enough by now just how tight Charlie would have clung to her, how they must have had to tear her off her mother. The whole picture of the brutality of the massacre flashed through my mind then, enraging me all over again. But not even that could take away how privileged I felt at that moment, to be there to witness the tenderness of their reunion.

trees, ambushing one another. I'd never seen them so relaxed and happy.

Sitting alone up on the rock, with Oona busy at her feeding and the orang-utans at play, I've got to admit that after a while I was beginning to feel ignored, abandoned even. It was as if they had forgotten all about me. So when I saw the mother climbing up the rock towards me, and bringing the little ones with her, I felt very grateful to her. She came to sit nearby, watching me, considering me. I sensed caution in her gaze, but approval too, almost as if the little ones had told her everything that had happened, about all we had been through together – which I knew was absurd, but I thought it anyway. And when after some time she reached out and touched my hand, I felt sure there was real affection in the gesture, and maybe even gratitude.

That evening the mother orang-utan climbed high into a tree, to make her sleeping nest, carrying all three of them. She went a great deal higher than I had ever managed. Again, I have to say I did feel excluded, which was ridiculous, I know, but it was why I left my rock, and went to lie down on the forest floor with Oona in the crook of her leg, braving the damp and the creepy-crawlies. I didn't want to be alone. I wanted to be close to her that night. I was missing my little family, and the intimacy of the sleeping nest.

But I had forgotten what good company Oona was, and what a good listener too. Never for one moment could I forget she was there. She was right beside me, the whole wonderful wrinkly, smelly, leathery bulk of her. I think I must have told her everything that night, all about Mister Anthony and Kaya and our escape from the cage, about the hunters and their dogs who came after us.

She kept touching me from time to time with the tip of her trunk, to reassure me perhaps; or maybe to reassure both of us, herself as well, that this had really happened, that we were together again, and not

of many reasons why I think I must have gone to sleep
that night with a laugh in my heart and a big big smile
on my face.

I was nudged awake next morning by Oona's trunk.
She wanted me to get up. The first thing I noticed was
that the jungle was filled with mist. Everything was lost
in it, except Oona and the looming shadow of the rock,
and the forest floor. Oona was unsettled, troubled by
something, tossing her head. She wanted to be on her
way, and she was in a hurry too. It was then that I began
to realise that there was something wrong about the
mist, something strange and unnatural. It didn't drift in
among the high canopy of the jungle as I'd seen it so
often before. Instead it hung low everywhere, clinging to
the trees. It was swirling all about us, snaking its way

through the forest. And it wasn't white, but almost yellow. It smelled different too. Now I knew it for what it was. It wasn't mist at all. It was smoke, drifting smoke. The jungle was on fire. The jungle was burning.

As I listened, I could hear, above me and around me, that all the invisible creatures of the forest were on the move. Whooping, cackling, cawing and screeching, they were fleeing for their lives. I could only hope that in among them somewhere were the mother orang-utan and the three little ones, and Other One.

I felt Oona's trunk come around me, pulling me in. She was urging me to mount. I needed little encouragement. I climbed up on to her neck. She was on the move at once, striding out, almost on the run already. She lifted her trunk and trumpeted. Then she was charging through the trees in full flight. Because everything had happened so fast, I hadn't been able to collect my thoughts. It was a while before I could, and when I did everything became horribly clear. I remembered then what Mister Anthony had told me, every chilling word: "I burn them down. I make a ruddy great bonfire of the forest."

We were careering through the trees now. It was all

toss, clutching desperately on to any folds of skin my
fingers could cling on to. But however fast Oona was
running from it, the smoke seemed always to be there,
all around us. In patches it was so dense now that I was
forced to hold my breath until we were out of it, and that
was terrifying, because once in the middle of a
suffocating whiteout like this, I would wonder if we'd
ever come out of it into clearer air beyond, whether I'd
ever be able to take a breath again.

In the end, with less and less good air to breathe, I
had to breathe in whatever there was, knowing even as
I was doing it, that I had to be taking in as much smoke
as air. I forced myself to make believe I was under
water, not to breathe at all. But of course, I had to. So
then I could only try not to breathe in deeply, not to gasp.

But I couldn't help myself. All I could do then was to try to control the coughing that was racking my whole body.

But the harder I tried to stop myself from coughing, the more I began to choke, and the giddier I was becoming. My whole head felt as if it was filling with smoke. I had my mouth closed. But somehow it seemed to be finding its way into me through my eyes, through my ears. I felt myself fainting, and for a few moments I tried to resist giving in to it. But there was nothing I could do about it. I fell heavily on to the forest floor – I remember that – and lay there for a few moments, gasping for breath. But on the ground I found there was at last some proper air to breathe. I looked up, and saw that Oona was coming back for me. Then she was trying to lift me, to get me to sit up.

With better air to breathe at last I recovered quickly. I had coughed and spluttered the smoke out of my lungs, and was thinking I was feeling just about strong enough now to climb back up on to Oona, when I felt myself being taken very firmly by the hand. I turned to see the mother orang-utan standing beside me, up on her two legs now, the three little ones clinging on to her.

The strength in her grip was so powerful that, like it or not, I had to get to my feet and go with her, go wherever

be hurting her dreadfully. It was obvious to me then that she could not cope on her own any longer with all three of them, that she needed my help, that she was asking for it. When I reached out a hand, there was barely a moment's hesitation before Bart grabbed it, and swung himself up on my shoulders, where he grasped my hair with his fists, and hung on, painfully. Tonk followed suit, without even being prompted, and nestled himself contentedly in the crook of my arm. Seemingly satisfied now, the mother orang-utan released my hand, and set off along the trail ahead of us walking three-legged, with Charlie's arms wrapped round her, and looking back all the while at me over her mother's shoulder.

I was unsure at first whether I should follow her or not. But when the orang-utan stopped and turned to look back at us, I was left in no doubt then she was waiting for us, that she meant us to follow her, and that she knew exactly where she was going. I had the distinct impression that she was taking charge. Oona seemed to sense it too for she began to move on along the trail following the orang-utan, and without stopping to offer me a ride either. I was a little disappointed at that, until I thought about it. I'd forgotten just how intelligent Oona was, how wise. It took me a while, but I soon understood that she must have known I was far better off where I was, down on the forest floor, out of the worst of the smoke.

Progress was slow now. We were having to travel at the leisurely pace of the mother orang-utan. And in places, where the trail was overgrown, or where it disappeared altogether, we were having to make our way through dense undergrowth. But at least, as we went, the air was becoming easier to breathe for all of us. Little Charlie was still suffering a bit. I could hear her struggling for breath sometimes, wheezing and coughing. We kept moving all through the heavy heat of the day. Then, towards evening a sudden breeze blew up, clearing the smoke at last.

When it came on to rain, when lightning crashed and

it would put out any fire Mister Anthony had started.

With the smoke gone, and weary of walking now, I begged a ride up on Oona. I had Bart and Tonk still attached, but as we rode, both of them seemed surprisingly unfazed either by Oona, or by their novel mode of transport. Ahead of us, the mother orang-utan plodded on with Charlie, showing no sign of slowing or stopping, even though the light was beginning to fail. There was an intrepid determination about her gait. Uphill, downhill, she just kept on going. I could see that she knew where she was going too. She wasn't just wandering aimlessly through the jungle. There could be no doubt about it. This was a trail she knew well. She was our pathfinder, she was showing us the way. We would stop when she was good and ready to stop, and not before.

But then, high above us, I heard and saw that Other One was still with us. He wasn't shadowing us though, he wasn't simply accompanying us. He was going on ahead of us, swinging through the trees, in front of the mother orang-utan. It was he that was leading us on our way, not her. I'd got it wrong. She was following him, and we were following both of them. More and more I was coming to think of Other One now as our guardian orang-utan, our guardian angel, that maybe he had been all along, from the very start.

It was nearly dark when we emerged at last out of the forest, into a different world, it seemed to me, and a lighter world too. We were being led along a narrow track, that wound steeply ever upwards, a sheer cliff face to one side of us. The track was only just wide enough for Oona. She trod gingerly, as surefooted and as careful as ever, and I was thankful for that, because I could see there was a drop on the other side of the trail, hundreds of feet down to a river and to the canopy of the forest below. As I looked back I could see all across the distant horizon the glow of a great fire, still burning bright despite the storm, and above it a blackened, apocalyptic sky, flickering with forked lightning

us. As we approached her I could see that she was standing outside the mouth of a cave, and making it quite plain that this was to be our refuge for the night.

Oona wasn't at all sure about this. She used her trunk as her antenna, satisfying herself that all was well before she ventured in. She took her time, and it was just as well. A sudden cloud of screeching bats came whirling out of the cave above our heads, a great roaring rush of them. This mass exodus seemed to go on and on. I was mightily relieved when it was over. Even after so long in the jungle, I still could never look at a bat without thinking of vampires. I knew they were only fruit bats, but they always alarmed me, particularly when they filled the air like this, in their thousands. Inside, the stench of the cave was so rank and foul that at first I could hardly bear to take a breath at all. But I got used to it.

The cave turned out to be a welcome resting place all the same, and not just for me either. I knew well enough that orang-utans loathed getting wet, and this at least would be dry. I liked dry too, even if the stench was foul. Oona seemed rather disappointed that there wasn't food about, but that didn't stop her searching. She found some in the end, as she always did. I could hear her exploring deep in the blackness of the cave. It sounded as if she was rubbing away with her trunk at the roof of the cave. Whatever it was she had discovered there — I thought it must be minerals or salt in the rock maybe — it kept her busy, and happy too. I could tell she was enjoying it, from the endless rumblings of satisfaction that echoed through the cave all night long.

I woke in the middle of the night to find Charlie crawling over me, her breath on my face, and the mother orang-utan sitting beside me holding my hand in hers. I thought then of Mum, of the night after we'd heard the news of Dad's death, how she'd lain beside me on my bed, how she'd held my hand all night. It was the first time that I'd thought about that in a very long time.

her again, whether or not I ever got out of this jungle, whether or not I ever got back home. And there was something else too. It occured to me that I wasn't sure I ever *wanted* to get back home at all.

At first light the mother orang-utan led the way out of the cave, down the treacherous track below the cliff, and then back down into the forest. For the first time now, I saw Other One down on the ground, walking on ahead of us all, way ahead – he liked to keep his distance wherever he was. He didn't only know the way, he also seemed to know where all the ripe fruit grew as well. Within a couple of hours we were feasting on figs again, but there was only one tree of them. So between all of us we had very soon stripped it bare.

We were just about ready to move on when the

mother orang-utan became suddenly agitated. She was swinging through the trees, calling out, searching frantically. I soon understood why. Charlie was nowhere to be seen. She wasn't playing in among the lower branches with Bart and Tonk where I'd last seen her. I wasn't too worried, not at first. Charlie was always wandering off from time to time – they all did. But once I'd thought about it, I realised that if her mother was alarmed, then she had good reason, and I should be worried too. So I was very relieved when, moments later, Charlie came scampering out of the undergrowth – until, that is, I saw that she was not alone.

Lumbering through the trees after her came a bear, not a bear like any other I had ever seen. It was small, and with a pale, pointed snout, but it was a bear nonetheless, and Charlie was running for her life. Only instinct could have made me do what I did. I ran at the bear waving my arms, shouting and screaming at the top of my voice. Taken by surprise, the bear stopped in his tracks and reared up on his hind legs, panting through his teeth. I could see his terrible claws, and the dark glint of anger in his eyes. For a few moments,

moments that seemed like a lifetime, the two of us stood there confronting one another, as Charlie ran squealing into her mother's arms. I could feel my heart pounding in my ears. I wanted to turn and run. I didn't stand there because I was brave. On the contrary. Sheer terror had simply rooted me to the spot. I couldn't move. Then Oona was there beside me, tossing her head and trumpeting. The bear didn't think twice then. He turned and ran off into the jungle.

After her trauma with the bear, Charlie stayed firmly attached to her mother for days. They turned out to be days of the worst heat and humidity I had ever known, sapping my strength, draining my energy. There was fruit enough, and some water from the leaves. But I longed for a stream to plunge into. I longed to be cool. It was late one afternoon that we emerged from the shadows of the forest, where at least we had been protected from the glare of the sun, on to the edge of a vast plantation of small palm trees, tens of thousands of them, millions of them maybe, that stretched away as far as the eye could see, rows and

rows of them, with little but bare brown earth in
between.

been alive with scents and colours and sounds. But
only palm trees grew here, in this new planet, nothing
else. There was no bird song, no clamour and chatter
of the jungle, no butterflies, no bees, none of the hum
and hubbub of the world to which I had become so
accustomed. In comparison to the jungle, this was, to
me, a dead place.

But Other One and the mother orang-utan seemed
to know their way even in this featureless plantation.
With Charlie still clinging round her neck, the mother
orang-utan followed along behind Other One, her
pace as constant as his, both of them tireless in their
determination to keep going. Oona would pause from
time to time to feed from the young palm trees, tearing
away the leaves to get at the soft hearts of them, which

were clearly delicious to her. But if ever Oona stopped too long to feed, the mother orang-utan would soon turn and give us one of her meaningful looks, and pretty quickly Oona would move on again. With no tall trees to shelter us, the sun was cruelly hot. I asked Oona to let me down, and made my own makeshift sunhat, from a huge palm frond she'd torn off. It worked too. Holding it over my head did pain my arm a bit after a while, but at least it served to protect me, and Bart and Tonk too, from the worst of the sun.

It took us many long days and nights to cross the desert of palm trees. I came to hate this barren place with a passion, and not just because the travelling seemed endless and monotonous, not just because I was always hungry, always thirsty – all of us were, except Oona. That was bad enough. But it was worry that was getting to me, worry that if Mister Anthony's hunters caught up with us now there would be nowhere for us to hide, nowhere for us to run to. The plantation seemed to go on for ever on all sides. I wondered if we would ever come out of it, and for the first time I began to question the wisdom of our guides. Other One and the mother orang-utan. They

again, not just strolling along as she had been. I was wondering why, when I looked out ahead of me from under my palm-frond hat and saw the great trees of the rainforest ahead of us in the distance. My heart rose. It seemed to me like I was coming home, and that's what it felt like too when we got there. I loved being back in the shade of it, searching for its fruits again, hidden in the safety of it. But best of all, after we had been back in the jungle only a short while, we found ourselves coming out into a clearing, a clearing which turned out to be the banks of a river, where the water was wide, and softly flowing, and dancing in sunlight. I thought it was the most welcome sight I'd ever seen.

Other One led all the orang-utans down to the

river's edge. I imagined that like Oona he must have had crocodiles on his mind, because like her he was being very cautious. He took his time, looking up and down the river, before allowing them to drink their fill. Oona and I joined them, but of course, for the two of us, water wasn't just for drinking, it was for washing in, and it was for messing around in. It was here that I lost my yellow T-shirt at last. I pulled it off before I dived in, and when I surfaced I saw Bart and Tonk playing at tug-of-war with it. I yelled at them, but it was no use. A few moments later it was in shreds. So now I would have to go naked, as they were, as every creature in the jungle was. It didn't bother me one bit. In fact I wondered why on earth I had gone on wearing it all this time. *Out of habit*, I thought, *out of nothing but habit*.

As we cavorted in the river, the orang-utans on the shore looked on, as if we were both completely mad. We would have stayed there for ever if we'd had our way, but the mother orang-utan would have none of it. They were moving on already. She kept turning and giving us that same long and meaningful look. "Come anxiety. I could see she was longing to jump down and run away, but never quite found the courage to do it. Her mother's arm came round her, and held her firmly.

Then, to my amazement, I realised that Other One and the mother orang-utan were picking the spot. They were going down into the river. They were going to swim, and not for fun, not to cool off, but to get to the other side. Until then I had never imagined that orang-utans could swim at all. The little ones had never shown any inclination to go anywhere near water, unless it was to drink, and even that took some persuasion. Other One was leading the way, and she was following. They were up to their necks in the river now, and swimming, Charlie clinging on, terrified. Oona looked as if she wanted to go too, so with Bart and Tonk hanging on to me and becoming ever more agitated, I shinned up her trunk and up on to her neck. Oona waited till we were settled, then made her way slowly down the bank and into the river. That was the moment, I remember, when I first began to feel strange. I thought it might be the water swirling all already, and standing there exhausted and dripping on the shore, Charlie still wailing in her mother's arms. In no time we were across the river too, clambering out of the water, up the bank the other side and into the forest beyond.

Almost as soon as we were in among the trees, I began to feel ill again. I remember the branches high above us rustling and shaking, that there was a lot of crashing about. It was as I was looking up into the trees to see what was up there, that I realised I couldn't see properly, that everything was blurred. I was finding it difficult to make any sense of what was going on around me. There were orang-utans up there, that much I knew by now, and not just one or two. There seemed to be dozens and dozens of them, and all swinging down into the lower branches to investigate us. But none of this seemed at all real to me. I felt I was drifting into a world of dreams. Yet at the same time I was sure I was still riding up on Oona, that Bart and Tonk were becoming more agitated than ever. They were choking me, and I was the hand. Other One seemed to have disappeared. I thought all this was impossible and odd, too odd to be real. But then, if I was dreaming, why shouldn't it be odd? Dreams were often odd.

"Mani?" said the woman, bending over the mother orang-utan so that their faces were almost touching. "It is you, Mani, isn't it? You've come back again. And you've another little one with you, I see. Not a year old yet by the looks of her. Is it all right if I say hello?" She put her other hand out then to Charlie, who took her finger, put it to her lips and sniffed it. Then she was looking up at me. I wasn't sure whether she was smiling at me or squinting into the sun.

"I think maybe you've got some explaining to do, Mani," she went on. "You know I always love to see you, Mani. I'm not complaining, not one bit, of course I'm not. I know how you like to come back from time to time when you feel the need, like a lot of my old girls. And that's fine by me. But would you mind telling me what on earth you've brought along with you this time? I mean, I'm sitting there on my porch, having a catnap in the evening sun, like I do. I open

266

my eyes, and what do I see? My old Mani back again, and with a baby too. But this time she's brought along

once that her smile wasn't one of politeness. It was a smile of genuine warmth, almost as if she knew me, had been expecting me. I liked her at once. I hated polite smiles, because I knew they were always empty. And I liked her also, because she looked so like Mum, a little older perhaps, but she smiled like Mum. She spoke like her. She was her. She had to be her. She was alive! I had found her!

I wanted to ask her so many questions, about how she had escaped the *tsunami*, about how it was that she'd known the mother orang-utan by name, how come the two of them had greeted each other like old friends. But somehow I couldn't speak the words. I couldn't make them come, and I couldn't work out why. And I wondered too why it was that when she was speaking I could only hear her as if she was speaking from somewhere far away. I could see her lips moving. I saw the concern on her face as she reached out her arms to me. I knew she was talking, but her voice seemed to be fading away all the time. The nausea was rising again in my stomach, and I felt a strange sense of detachment coming over me, as if I was leaving my body altogether. I longed only to fall asleep now. I tried all I could to resist, because I knew that if I gave in to it, I would be leaving Mum and Oona for ever, and I would be dead.

There was nothing I could do about it though. I was going to fall. My last thought was that Bart and Tonk must somehow have known it, because I could feel them hugging me even tighter, their fingernails digging into my skin so hard that it hurt. I heard myself crying out, and then I was falling into a whirlpool, a whirlpool of emptiness.

Sanctuary

 had no idea of the passing of time, nor of anything much, only that I must be ill, because when I was conscious, I knew that I was in bed and unable to move. I was either pouring sweat or shivering with cold. There seemed to be many different voices in the room around me, but nothing they said made any sense to me. I wasn't even sure if they were real voices anyway, or just

inside my head. I wondered often if I was going to die, if this was what dying was like, but I felt so sick and weak I didn't much care one way or another.

I tried all I could to wake up properly and discover where I was, to find out to whom the voices belonged, and to understand what they were saying. But for most of the time I lay there unable to escape this strange limbo I was living in, somehow unable to reach the real world beyond, the world I remembered, that I hoped would be full of the faces and places I knew. I think I always believed I would get there, but I wasn't at all sure that when I did I would find myself in the living world, or in the world of the dead.

I woke one morning and saw there was sunlight streaming in through an open window beside my bed. I was lying in a small room. Above me there was a wooden ceiling and a paper globe lampshade like the one in the hallway back home. It was swaying gently. I turned my face towards the window because I could feel there was a cooling breeze wafting through. I breathed it in deep, so relieved I had woken up at last, and overjoyed to find myself in the land of the living.

I only really began to make some sense of anything when I saw Oona's trunk reaching in through the

or some part of her, was there at my window. That cheered me so much, lifted my heart every time. What I could be quite certain of by now was that when I next woke, Oona would be standing guard out there, waiting for me, and I knew she'd always be there while I was asleep too. It might be her trunk searching me out again, or her weepy eye looking in on me, or maybe it would be the great pink-grey bulk of her blocking the window. I didn't mind. It would be Oona.

Sometimes, when I woke, I found that I had been propped up on a pile of pillows. I could often see past Oona then, and catch glimpses of the wide green lawn with low wooden huts all around. I remembered this place. Beyond them was the forest, and the sounds of the forest. There were comings and goings outside that

I could make no sense of at all. Strange games were being played out on the lawn. One moment it would be empty all together, except for a strutting peacock or maybe the occasional orang-utan – once or twice. I did think I recognised Other One sitting there at the edge of the forest – and the next moment it seemed that the whole place became some kind of nursery or playgroup for tiny orang-utans, all with someone to look after them, a minder or a nurse, and these women were always dressed in white.

The smaller orang-utans, I noticed – and it made me smile each time I saw it – were wearing nappies. Some were being fed from a bottle, but mostly they would be playing, rolling and tumbling and clambering over their minders. Of course I looked at once for Bart and Tonk and Charlie in among them, but if they were there, I didn't recognise them. There were far too many of them, and they all looked so alike.

I would see a few older orang-utans mooching around too, and usually the lady in the straw hat was out there somewhere, crouched down among the little ones maybe, or sometimes sitting cross-legged on the lawn, and playing with the older ones, talking to them. Once or twice I thought I

to her, and she might have been Charlie, but I couldn't be sure. I couldn't be sure of anything. This whole orang-utan nursery was so bizarre, so unlikely that sometimes I wondered whether what I was seeing was real at all, or whether it might all be part of some fantastical dream.

But I never doubted for one moment as I lay there that Oona was real, and that she was there outside the window. Even by night, when I couldn't see her, I could hear her rumbling away, groaning and chomping on her food, and farting. Farting she did a lot. It was my constant lullaby and I loved it. Every time she did it, I absolutely knew that Oona could not be part of some crazy dream, because I could smell her. It was her constant presence, the reassuring sound of her, and that familiar smell of her, that began bit by bit to make me feel alive, and part of a real world again – however improbable and strange this new world might seem to be.

Sometimes I could smell lavender too. There were early mornings when I'd wake up to see the woman in the straw hat sitting on a chair beside me, reading a book or writing. Sometimes I still believed that she was Mum, because Mum too had often smelled of lavender. But then she would speak. She had a lilt in her voice that wasn't at all how Mum spoke, and I would know then that it couldn't be her after all. And I would remember that Mum was dead in the *tsunami*. It hurt my heart to realise it, but it was true. This was not Mum.

I longed to talk to this woman in the straw hat. I still didn't even know who she was. She'd talk to me, take my temperature, tell me how much better I was looking. She'd feed me, and bathe me, but I was still too weak to utter a single word to her. But with every day that passed I was making more and more determined efforts to communicate with her. She could see that I was, and would encourage me. But the effort always proved to be too much, and I would find myself drifting back to sleep again. It made me so angry and frustrated every time I

what I dreaded. It would begin well enough. I'd be riding through the jungle high on Oona. Everything was fine. I'd be frolicking with her in the river. That was fine too. Then I'd find myself up in a sleeping nest high in a tree, with Charlie and Bart and Tonk crawling all over me, and they'd be wearing nappies, and the lady in the straw hat would somehow be up there in the nest too. And all that was fine, and funny too.

But then without warning there was fire burning all around us and I couldn't breathe for the smoke, and I'd be looking everywhere for Dad, stumbling through the smoke, but I could never find him. I was running then through the jungle and the hounds were after me. Sooner or later I would find myself on the beach, still running, and the towering green wave was coming in, and I would see Mum trying to escape it, but it curled over her and she disappeared into it, and the green water was coming into my mouth and I knew I was drowning too.

That was always the moment when I woke up. I'd wake choking, and the woman would be there, her arm around me, giving me water to drink. I couldn't tell her, but the last thing I wanted to swallow was water. I'd taste it and discover there was no salt in it, and only then did I really understand it had all been a dream. But at the same time I'd also remember that so much of the dream had been true.

The day came when I woke and felt I could sit up on my own if I tried. So I did, I managed it. And moments later when the woman in the straw hat came in carrying a tray, she looked so surprised. "Well you certainly took your time, didn't you? Weeks you've been lying there," she said. "Do you feel like a bit of breakfast? Will you be able to feed yourself now?"

"I think so," I replied, surprised at the sound of my own voice, surprised it was working.

She put the tray down on the chair, and sat down on

the bed beside him. "You gave us all quite a fright, you know. But the doctor was right. He said it would take a

forehead in much the same way as Mum used to do. At that moment the end of Oona's trunk curled in through the window.

"For goodness' sake, will you get that wiggly thing out of here and let the boy eat!" she said, pushing the trunk away. "Do you know that elephant has hardly budged since the very first day you came in here? And what an entrance that was! Naked as a newborn babe you were, did you know that? You gave me one look from up there on that elephant, went as white as milk and just tumbled off. Nearly flattened me you did when you fell. Ever since you arrived she's been moping around out there. She goes down to the river for a drink from time to time, but that's all she does, that's as far as she goes. We've had to bring her all her food because she wouldn't go and get it herself. I thought, to start with, she was just a lazy old thing."

"Oona," I told her. "She's called Oona, and she's not lazy"

"Pretty name," she said. "And I know now that Oona's not lazy, not at all, of course I do. She wouldn't leave your side, that's the truth of it. She'd have starved herself to death rather than leave you, honest to God she would. All very noble, I'm sure, but do you know, young man, how much an elephant eats? Tons and tons of the stuff, I'm telling you, and we've had to fetch it for her, every last leaf of it. I mean it's been nonstop, and what's more we've had not a word of thanks from her."

She got up and lifted the tray on to my lap. "Here. Breakfast. The ladies make it up specially for you, so you eat it now. They've taken quite a shine to you. We all have, if I'm honest. Orang-utans we're used to, but a boy – well, you're the first." She pushed Oona's trunk away again. "Get out of it, will you!" And she wagged her finger at me. "And don't you be letting her have any of it, do you hear me? Promise me now."

But I wasn't interested in food at all. I had other

things on my mind. "Where am I?" I asked her. "What is this place? All these orang-utans, and you…"

off the forest floor, the doctor said. You're over it. But you must eat." She smoothed my hair again. "I'm glad you came, Will. We don't get many visitors out here."

"You called me Will," I said. "How d'you know my name?"

"Let's just say that it's a long story. I'll tell you soon enough, when you're better, when you're fit and well again." And that was all she would tell me.

I forced myself to eat, because I wanted to get better, because I knew she was right about that. But for days and days I had no real appetite. I didn't have the strength yet to be out of bed for long, but I was getting bored just lying there talking to Oona through the window all the time. I wanted to be up and about. So one morning I ventured down the steps and walked out on to the lawn to be with the minders and their little orang-utans. In fact, they seemed to me to be more like foster mothers than nurses or minders. In no time at all the orang-utans became accustomed to my being there.

Oona didn't come with me – she seemed to know when to keep her distance. I sat down, and at once they were right there, half a dozen of them, clambering all over me. And then I saw them – Bart and Tonk running across the grass towards me. They were in nappies now, and each of them had a foster mother of his own in hot pursuit. Best of all was when Charlie appeared on the lawn with her mother. She scampered over to me at once, and soon displaced the others, sitting herself on my head and grooming me, like the old days. Mani didn't seem to mind. She'd just stay sitting nearby, keeping an eye on things. And that was when I noticed Other One sitting in the shade on the edge of the forest, watching over us all, but still keeping himself to himself.

After that I was out there on the lawn whenever I could be. If I wasn't there I felt I was missing out. Charlie was always full of beans, but I could see that there were many others who were listless and withdrawn, clutching on tight to their foster mothers as if they'd never let go. I was particularly drawn to these

on. To be trusted, completely trusted, I was learning, is the best of feelings.

Oona would sometimes wander over to remind me she was there, that perhaps it was about time I paid some attention to her now. I couldn't walk far yet, so I'd sit on the steps of the house, hold her trunk and talk. She would snuffle at my hair, and do her groaning and her rumbling. She was happy.

These were peaceful times and healing days for me. My appetite and my strength were growing every day. I got to talk with many of the orang-utans' foster mothers, many of whom could speak a little English. But whether or not we understood one another, I had the feeling that I had been 'adopted' by all of them. Sitting among them on the lawn I began to understand what a truly amazing place this was. I was living on an island sanctuary in the jungle surrounded by the river, in an orphanage for orang-utans, set up by the woman in the straw hat, whom they all called Dr Geraldine.

As I had supposed, all these infant orang-utans had a foster mother, who never left their sides. They fed them, played with them, taught them to climb trees, slept with them at night, and loved them. Little by little, they were helping me to make some sense of everything that had happened, how it was that Mani had brought us here for instance, how she herself had been one of their orphaned orang-utans. Dr Geraldine had rescued her years ago, they told me – she'd been discovered caged up and locked away in someone's garage – and had grown up in this place, and lived like all the others with a human adoptive mother. Then, once Mani had been taught to climb, once she could feed herself and fend for herself, she had been released back into the jungle, but to begin with, only as far as the island itself, where the orang-utans would be safe, where Dr Geraldine could keep a watchful eye on them to see how they were managing.

After some while living in this 'university of the jungle', as Dr Geraldine called it, they'd be taken away

enough, so far as I could understand, provided they didn't stray from the reserve, and provided that hunters didn't trespass on the reserve and kill them, or kidnap them, or burn them out. But this was happening all the time, they said. That much I knew only too well.

The orphanage, I learned, had been built almost single-handed by Dr Geraldine herself. She had saved hundreds, maybe thousands of orang-utans, over the last twenty years or more, sometimes risking her own life to rescue them, they said. To begin with, she'd tried to care for them all herself, but very soon there were just too many of them. So she'd gone into the villages up and down the river to recruit the helpers she needed, to mother the little orang-utans, and to try to teach them what their orang-utan mothers would have taught them, until they were ready to be released back into the wild.

Dr Geraldine hadn't spoken to me herself about any of this. She had been kind, kindness itself, but she was sometimes away for a day or two – I didn't know where, and she didn't say. When she was home, she seemed always busy and preoccupied, tired too, and because of this I didn't find her at all easy to talk to, not to begin with. She was accustomed to silence in her home, I could tell that, so I didn't feel I could interrupt it with my questions – and I had plenty of them. Everything I knew about her, about this place, I'd found out from the foster mothers, who, like the orang-utans themselves, so very obviously trusted and adored her.

One evening out on the lawn, one of them was singing her praises yet again. "Without Doctor Geraldine," she was saying, "without her, these creatures would have no life, no future, no hope."

"And without Doctor Geraldine we would have no work either," said another. "We love the work as much as we love her. She's an angel for the orang-utans, and for us too.

"Enough of your tittle-tattling," came a voice from above me. "An angel I most certainly am not." I looked up to see Dr Geraldine standing there in her hat. It occurred to me then that I'd never once seen her without her hat on, inside or outside the house, and I wondered what she'd look like without it.

She held out her hand to help me up on to my feet. "I thought if you felt strong enough, Will, if you're up to it, you might like to come for a walk with me. Not far, just down to the river and back. It's my constitutional, my evening stroll. Be good to have company."

We walked for some time in silence down the path, Oona following along some distance behind, Other One alongside her. The two were often together these days, I noticed. I asked about him then, about Other One, whether like Mani he had been one of her orphaned orang-utans. "No," she told me. "He's a bit of a strange one, an interloper, you might say. He comes and he goes as he pleases. Sometimes I think he's inspecting us, checking us out to see if we're doing things right. I think he approves; I certainly hope so."

The walk was quite a bit further than I had gone before, and I got tired quickly. So I was happy to reach

peaceful place in the world for me. It's where I think all my big thoughts, and a lot of my little ones too, come to that."

I wasn't really listening. I was staring at her head. She had a large bald patch, from her forehead up to the crown of her head. I could see the skin was puckered and scarred. "Ah, that," she said, touching the place. "Not a pretty sight. You make enemies doing this kind of work, Will. You know what's funny? It was a present from someone I don't even know, one of the big boys in Jakarta who are burning down the forests, killing the orang-utans, selling off the babies. One night, it'd be maybe ten years ago now, they came and tried to burn us out. They very nearly succeeded too. My hair caught fire as I was running out of the house. It's a secret I like to keep under my hat, if you see what I'm saying."

She laughed a little at that, but I didn't. "But there're worse things than losing your hair, Will," she said. "You know what? All it did was make me more angry, more determined. They didn't stop us then, and they won't stop us now, not ever, not while I'm alive and kicking. We've saved quite a few orang-utans – not enough, never enough. But we're going to save a lot more, because we have to. Shall I tell you something, Will? If we don't save them, and if we don't save the rainforests where they live, then five years from now there won't be any orang-utans left in the wild. That's the truth of it."

"Does it hurt?" I asked her, unable to take my eyes off her scar.

"No, not at all," she said. "Not any more – well only when I think about it maybe. But that's not at all what I brought you here to tell you. I want to tell you another truth. I've wanted to for a long time, and now I can." She reached out then and took my hand in hers. "You remember you asked me once, when you first turned up, how it was that I knew your name? The truth is, that I knew a lot more than just your name, Will. I know how had been drowned in the *tsunami* on Boxing Day 2004, and his father, their only son, had been killed in the army in Iraq only a short time before. You don't forget it when people tell you such sad and terrible things. They showed me the leaflet with your photo, Will. When I first saw you, you looked a little different, of course – shorter hair, younger maybe, but quite recognisable. And besides, there aren't many boys like you, just wandering around the rainforest with an elephant. I knew about the elephant too. They had some hope you must still be alive, because of a story they'd heard more than once while they'd been out here looking for you, a story about an elephant, a beach elephant, that was seen taking off into the jungle as the wave was coming in, with a boy on her back, a boy with fair hair. These two wonderful people had been searching for you for months, all along the coast, and now inland too, dropping off their leaflets everywhere they went, and asking if anyone might possibly have seen you, or heard of you. When they'd gone I couldn't stop thinking about them, about how determined they were to find you. They had so much love in them for you, so much faith and belief. They never gave up on you. They were willing you to be alive. And you were too, weren't you?"

lot of things I don't understand. The *tsunami* was over a year ago now. You've been gone all that time, you and that elephant. How on earth did you survive out there? That's what I want to know. But then maybe you don't want to talk about it. That's fine. You don't need to tell me, not if you don't want to."

But I *did* want to. I don't know why, but suddenly I wanted to tell her everything. So I did, and as I did, I felt I was living it all again, from that first stampede up the beach into the forest to the day we'd swum across the river and reached her orang-utan orphanage. Dr Geraldine listened in silence all the while, as darkness came down around us. The memories were so vivid to me, and often so painful, that at times I found it difficult to go on. At moments like this she'd squeeze my hand tight. Every time she did so, it reminded me of how a long time ago, a whole lifetime ago it seemed, Mum had done much the same thing, and for much the same sort of reason too. After I'd finished Dr Geraldine asked me no questions, and I was glad of that. I'd said all I wanted to say, and I think she knew it. The two of us sat there for a while, listening to the river running by, to the orchestra of the jungle all around, to Oona groaning and grunting, slapping the river with her trunk.

"Will?" Dr Geraldine said, putting her arm round me. "There's one more thing I've got to tell you. On the leaflet your grandparents left, under the photo of you with your name and your description, there was a telephone number to ring if anyone found you. That first day you arrived I tried it, but either I couldn't get through, or the number didn't answer. I don't know. It's taken me a long while to find them. But I tracked them down in the end through the Red Cross. I finally spoke to your grandmother and your grandfather only a few days ago, Will. They'd been away, still looking for you all this time. They'd only just got back home. If you could have heard them, Will, the relief and the joy in their voices. It was the best phone call I've ever had to make in my life. They're on their way back out here

Elephant's child

spent the next few days trying to put Grandma and Grandpa out of my mind, trying to forget they were coming, and then feeling guilty about it. I knew it was wrong to feel as I did about them. On the one hand, I really was looking forward to seeing them again. But the trouble was that I couldn't help thinking they were part of a world I had left behind, that I wanted to forget, and

had come to believe I would never see again. What was worse still, was that I knew all too well that they weren't just coming to see me for a visit. As Dr Geraldine had said, they were coming to take me home, away from Oona, from all the orang-utans, from the jungle. That was the thought I couldn't stand.

Every morning when I woke up, instead of feeling overjoyed at the thought of this happy reunion with Grandpa and Grandma, as I knew I should have been, I would be hoping that this would not be the day they arrived. I decided there was only one thing for it: I would live every single day I had left in this place to the full, as if it was the last. I was feeling better in myself every day, and so was able to busy myself about the place, filling feeding bottles, cutting up fruit in the kitchens for the orang-utans, helping out with the laundry, fetching and carrying supplies from the jetty, playing with Charlie, Tonk, Bart and the others on the lawn, and at night sometimes sleeping with the little orang-utans and their foster mothers on the floor of the dormitory. I'd often wake to find that either Charlie or Tonk or Bart, all three of them sometimes, had crept over during the night and were lying on me or beside me, snuggled up to me.

shadowing us all the way. Oona never liked being left out of anything, and where Oona went, Other One went too. When Dr Geraldine said she was getting a crick in her neck with Oona and Other One trailing us all day, I suggested we both hitched a ride on Oona. I knew that Oona would be more than happy to oblige.

Dr Geraldine had ridden an elephant before, she told me, but not for a while, so it took her some time to relax. But the more we rode, the more she was enjoying it. We hardly walked at all after that; Other One was our path-finder or our shadow, sometimes walking, sometimes swinging through the trees above us.

These long rides into the jungle were always silent. Dr Geraldine was very strict about it. We rarely talked, hardly a word. As she had explained to me, it was important that we disrupt the lives of the orang-utans as little as possible. The whole point of the orang-utans' time in 'the university of the jungle' was to persuade them not to rely any more on human contact. So the less they saw and heard of us the better. They had to learn to keep their distance from people for their own safety, to become wild again.

Dr Geraldine had to keep an eye on them, but at the same time remain as unobtrusive as possible. It was, she once told me, the most difficult decision she had to make, to know when the time was right for an orang-utan to be taken from 'the university' and released into the reserve. Do it too early, when they weren't yet ready for it, when they couldn't cope properly, and she could be condemning them to death. Once out there in the reserve, they were on their own.

In the evenings I would often sit down with Dr Geraldine on the steps of the house after supper, and we'd talk. We talked more and more these days. Other One would be off in the jungle somewhere by this time, up in his sleeping nest. But Oona was never far away of course. "You know something, Will," Dr Geraldine said

to me one evening, "I think I might have
to change my mind about that elephant

course they are. She's a new thing for them – and
let's face it, she's a big thing too. I don't know what it is
about her, but wherever she goes, that elephant, she
radiates a calm and a peace. I'm not imagining that,
am I?"

"No," I said. "You're not."

The very next day we had ample proof of that. We
were riding up on Oona, through the forest, Other One
swinging through the trees above us, when we saw a
huge male orang-utan walking towards us on all fours.
From the way he was walking, from the way he was
looking right at us, rolling his great shoulders as he
came, it was obvious he meant business. He was not
looking at all pleased at this intrusion. I thought I might
have caught a distant glimpse of a big male like this a

while back, crashing about high above us in the canopy, his voice booming through the forest. But this was the first time I'd come face to face with one this big, this close, down on the forest floor. Dr Geraldine put a hand on my shoulder. "This is Ol," she whispered in my ear. "He's fine when he's fine. So we just keep very still. That way we keep him fine."

It reminded me of the meeting with the tiger all that time ago. Oona stood quite still, and for a while so did the orang-utan. He had huge black cheek-flaps, deep piercing eyes, and a golden beard, *like a Viking's beard*, I thought. Oona looked down at him quite unperturbed, then as if he wasn't there at all, began to browse for food. Meanwhile, the orang-utan was showing no overt signs of aggression, but he was also showing no sign of moving. He seemed to be making it quite clear that he would move when he felt like it and not before, however big this new giant was. He sat down for a while, scratching his ear, and then looked the other way, very deliberately ignoring us, making out he hadn't a care in the world.

After some minutes of this charade, once he was

satisfied everything was as it should be, I suppose, that Oona was neither a threat nor a challenge, that he'd

Geraldine told me about how she had discovered Ol several years before, only a couple of months old, sitting next to the charred body of his mother after a jungle fire, burnt, half starved and covered in sores. I remembered then that photograph in the magazine back home, saw again in my head the little orang-utan clinging to the top of the charred tree. It could have been Ol. "He won't ever go back into the wild," she went on, her voice catching as she spoke. "He's too traumatised, even now. He always will be."

She was turning her face away, so that I couldn't see she was crying. "Will you look at me?" she said, wiping away her tears. "Crying my stupid eyes out. I ask you, Will, how's that going to help anyone? It's not because I feel sorry for myself, I promise you. I'm just angry. I need eyes and ears in the jungle. I need to be out there, to be on the spot, to stop the burning and killing before it happens. And if the worst did happen, then at least I could be there quickly. I could fetch them back. I could save them before it was too late. So many of them die, Will, and there's no one out there to help them. But I can't be out in the jungle, and back here at the same time. It makes me so angry that I can do so little."

"It's not so little," I told her. "When you save one of their lives, like you do, I think it's like saving a whole world each time." I felt her hand reaching out, holding mine and squeezing it tight.

"We make a fine team, you and I," she said. "I'm going to miss you when you go. So will everyone here, that elephant most of all."

"You know I don't want to go, don't you?" I told her.

"I know," she replied. "I've got eyes. I've got a brain too. I know what you've been thinking, Will."

"What if I asked them if I could stay?" I asked her.

"You could ask, but you'd be breaking their hearts if you did," she told me. "I can't tell you what to do, Will. You'll have to make up your mind for yourself. But I will say this, and it's maybe something you should think about. Nothing in the world matters to those two

felt like, do I? And then they get a phone call from me to tell them you're alive after all. You're right when you say that every one of those little orang-utans is a whole world. And that's what you are to your grandparents, Will. You're their whole world. Whatever you do, you mustn't forget that."

All that night I lay there trying to reconcile myself to the idea that Dr Geraldine had been right about Grandma and Grandpa, and that I had no choice but to leave with them when they came for me. After all Grandpa and Grandma had done to find me, I couldn't disappoint them. I had to go back to England, to my old life. But trying to convince myself I was looking forward to it was another matter. It wasn't that I didn't want to see them. Of course I did, although I was becoming increasingly nervous about it. And most certainly it wasn't that I didn't like the idea of making my home with them back on the farm in Devon – that's what I presumed would happen. Nowhere could be better. It was simply that I didn't want to leave this place. I did not want to leave Oona, or Dr Geraldine, or the orang-utans, or the jungle.

It did not make it any easier, as I lay there on my bed, that the music of the jungle seemed to be particularly loud and insistent that night, as if every creature out there was calling to me, begging me to stay. And neither did it help that I could hear Oona outside my window all night, groaning away. She kept reaching in with her trunk to touch me – it was to remind me she was there, I was sure of it. I had no doubt at all that this was her way of asking me not to leave her.

Unable to sleep, I went and sat out on the steps to clear my head. When Oona came wandering over, and stood there looking down at me with the moon in her eye, her trunk exploring my hair, I knew that I couldn't keep silent, that I'd have to tell her everything, all about

Grandpa and Grandma and how they'd been looking for me all this while, that now they were on their way, and

forget anything, do they?" I couldn't speak any more. My tears wouldn't let me.

I leaned my head against her trunk and hugged it, hugged her. "Sometimes, Oona," I told her, "sometimes I really feel like I'm your child, like I'm an elephant's child." We stayed together until first light, until we heard Dr Geraldine humming to herself as she got up. Oona wandered off then, looking resigned and disconsolate, no more happy about the idea of the parting to come than I was.

Breakfast that morning was a silent affair. I think we had said all there was to be said the night before, and each of us knew what the other was thinking, so there was no point in talking. I kept reading the poster on the wall. I'd seen it before, but hadn't taken that much notice of it. Until now, I think I'd been more interested in the collage of photos of orang-utans all around it.

> *'When all the trees*
> *have been cut down,*
>
> *when all the animals*
> *have been hunted,*
>
> *when all the waters*
> *are polluted,*
>
> *when all the air is*
> *unsafe to breathe,*
>
> *only then will you*
> *discover you cannot*
> *eat money.'*
> *(Cree prophecy, North America.)*

I was still thinking about that as, later that morning, Dr Geraldine and I were riding out again into the jungle to check on the orang-utans, accompanied as usual by Other One, and this time by Mani and Charlie too. But

where she wanted, and at her own pace too, faster, slower, whatever she felt like, and there was nothing I could do about it.

She kept tossing her head, a sure sign she was not happy. And from time to time she would stop suddenly, unexpectedly, and it wasn't to feed either. She'd just stand there listening. I thought it could be that Ol was shadowing us, following along the trail behind us, or swinging through the trees, that his invisibility was unnerving her. I kept looking for him, listening for him. Other One was there, plodding along with Mani and Charlie, and they were all calm enough. There was no sign of Ol. I could see no reason at all why Oona should be like this.

When the thunder rattled and echoed about the sky,

when the lightning crackled, and the rains came down,
I thought that might be enough in itself to explain
Oona's strange behaviour, that she must have felt the
storm coming. But when the storm had passed over, she

was just as difficult, just as unpredictable, tugging and tearing impatiently at the branches, but never once stopping to feed properly on the move, as she usually did. I came to the conclusion that she wasn't frightened,

that there was nothing to be frightened of. But she was upset, as upset as I'd ever seen her. Dr Geraldine kept asking me what the matter with her was, and I couldn't tell her. "Maybe she's unwell," she said. "Maybe she's eaten something that didn't agree with her."

I was still wondering if she could be right about that, when we reached the river on the far side of the island. It looked to me as if Oona wasn't going to stop at all, that she was going to wade right in. But she did stop, at the very last moment, and stood there on the bank for a while, gazing out across the river at the jungle on the far side. Then she turned, and began to walk very slowly, reluctantly, back the way we had come. She took her time, not walking so much as meandering, so we didn't come out of the forest and back to the orphanage until the light was fading. That was when I saw them.

On the steps of Dr Geraldine's house sat Grandpa and Grandma, a suitcase beside them. Grandpa was wearing the same tweed jacket and flat cap he always wore, and Grandma, dressed in one of her flowery dresses, was fanning herself with her hat. They looked older, smaller, more shrunken than I remembered, and greyer too. Oona stopped where she was when she saw them. She lifted her trunk in the air and tossed her

could barely speak.

"Course it's him," Grandpa said, walking straight up to me. "Who else would it be?" He put his arms round me then, and held me. Both of us were choking back our tears. "I always knew you were alive, Will. I always knew." Then he was holding me at arm's length, and looking me up and down. "You're a sight for sore eyes, Will," he said. "You've grown too. Young man almost. Nearly as tall as me, you are. Isn't he, Grandma?" But Grandma had her hands over her face and was sobbing. I went to her at once and hugged her. She felt thinner than I had remembered her.

"What did I do to you, Will?" she cried. "What did I do?" I felt her head heavy on my shoulder. "If I hadn't sent you off like that, on that stupid, stupid holiday. If only I hadn't done it, she would still be with us. You'd still have a mother."

"She blames herself, Will," Grandpa said. "Ever since, she's always blamed herself."

Until that moment I think I had always been a little frightened of Grandma. But now I knew she needed comforting, that I was the only one who could do it. I chose my words carefully.

"You're wrong, Grandma," I told her. "It was the tidal wave that killed Mum, not you. I don't know who made that happen, Grandma, but you didn't."

Dr Geraldine waited for a while before she came over and shook them both by the hand. "I'm the one who phoned you. I don't know if you remember me, but I'm Geraldine," she said. "Welcome back. It's lovely to see you again."

"We remember you, of course we do. And we remember this place too, so well." Grandma was still trying to collect herself as she spoke. "We remember the little orang-utans. We went to lots and lots of places along the river, delivering those leaflets. But this one we never forgot. We've talked about it ever since, haven't we, Grandpa?"

But Grandpa wasn't listening. He was looking up at Oona, who had wandered across towards us. "So this is

you." He said it softly, looking her right in the eye. He turned back to me then. "Don't hardly need a tractor any more do you, Will, not with a giant like this for a friend?" He laughed at that. I knew he was only laughing to hide his emotion, but even so I couldn't laugh with him. I couldn't even smile, and that troubled me.

I felt troubled all evening as the four of us sat eating our supper in Dr Geraldine's house. "We've looked you up on Google, Geraldine," Grandpa was saying. "Will taught us to do all that. You remember, Will? That's how we found out all about the orang-utans and the orphanage. To be honest, the last time we came, I don't think we understood much of what was going on here. We had our minds on other things, I suppose. Quite a set-up you've got, Geraldine. Must have taken a lot of work, and… well, dedication. Yes, that's the word I was looking for, dedication. Marvellous what you've done. Marvellous."

Grandma seemed to have quite recovered her composure by now, and was becoming more and more her old self as the evening went on, more the Grandma I remembered. She was doing most of the talking, interrupting Grandpa, contradicting him. It was all very familiar. Only now I didn't have Mum there to wink back at me across the table in solidarity. I missed her suddenly, achingly, and was finding it very difficult to concentrate on what Grandma was telling me.

"Will?" she was saying, "Will, are you listening to me? We've got so much to tell you, about the farm, about your new school. It's difficult to know where to begin. But it's all going to be fine, you'll see. I've arranged everything. Your old room's waiting for you, just as you left it."

I could hear Oona rumbling and groaning outside, letting me know she was there, reminding me, not allowing me to forget. I was hoping she would fart. It would be the perfect moment, I thought. Amazingly, just as I was thinking that, she did it, one of her longest and

"Oona," I told her. "It's only Oona, Grandma. It's how she talks."

"Oh dear, oh deary dear. She gave me a turn, quite a turn. Now, as I was saying," she went on, "before the elephant interrupted, everything will be just as you want it, Will. Do you know what I did before we came away? I rang up the local school and told them all about you. The head teacher sounded very nice. She can't wait to have you there. They're over the moon. Lovely uniform too – striped blazers, maroon and black. Very smart, isn't it, Grandpa? You'll like it, Will. Before you know it you'll have lots of new friends. You're quite a celebrity back home in England, you know. In fact you're quite a celebrity all over the world, come to think of it."

"What do you mean?" I asked. I couldn't understand what she was talking about.

"Well, you've been in all the newspapers, dear, *Sun*, *Mirror*, *The Times* even. Front page too. We've saved all the press cuttings, every one of them. You're big news. It's a big story, all about how that elephant ran off with you when the *tsunami* came in, and about you being lost in the jungle all this time. 'Little Tarzan' they're calling you. And when we get to the airport tomorrow, there'll be photographers, Will, dozens of them. Isn't that exciting? I wanted to bring them here to see you, you know, with all the orang-utans and the elephant; but Grandpa said no, said you'd need a bit of time to get used to things. I'm still not sure he was right. But anyway, we've got to be back by six o'clock tomorrow evening for a press conference at the airport. The embassy in Jakarta have arranged it all. Very nice man, the ambassador, wasn't he Grandpa?"

"Tomorrow?" I said. "We're going tomorrow?"

"Yes, dear. We must," she replied, reaching across then, and touching my hair. "Your hair, it's the same colour as

your father's, Will – a little lighter maybe, but that'd be
the sun. He had his long like yours – well, not as long

Her voice was trembling now. "And they're all sons,
and brothers, daughters, and husbands, every one of
them. Don't mind me," she said, wiping her eyes, "I'll
be fine in a moment." Grandpa put his hand on her
shoulder to comfort her. It was a while before she
could bring herself to go on. "Where was I? Oh yes.
Your hair, Will. I mean, we'll have to get you a haircut,
you know, before you go back to school."

"Why?" I said, and I spoke sharply, more sharply
than I'd intended. "I don't need a haircut, Grandma."

Everyone was looking at me. I knew I'd upset her. I
said nothing else all evening, because I didn't trust
myself.

That last night I went to sit down outside on the step
with Oona. I couldn't sleep – I didn't want to. I think I

talked to her all night long, speaking all my thoughts and feelings as they came tumbling into my head, as I always had. There was never anyone else I could talk to like that, and I knew there never would be. I wanted that night to last for ever, for morning never to come. But it did, all too soon.

We had a hurried breakfast together the next morning, but I didn't feel like eating a thing. Oona was waiting for me outside all the while. When the time came to say goodbye, it felt to me as if I was betraying her, abandoning her. All I wanted to do was get it over quickly. I couldn't bear to look at her. I just closed my eyes and hugged her trunk. "I want you to stay here, Oona," I whispered. "If you come down to the boat with me, I'll cry. And I don't want to cry." When I opened my eyes, I saw Other One at the edge of the forest, watching.

I left Oona and walked away, down towards the jetty. Everyone was there, everyone who worked at the orphanage. They were all lined up there, all the foster mothers with the little orang-utans in their arms. I found Mani walking alongside me, and then Charlie was there

too, holding my hand all the way, gripping it tight. I
wanted to stop and say goodbye to Bart and Tonk, but I

me, that I changed my mind. As Dr Geraldine came to
say her goodbyes, I stood up on tiptoe and whispered to
her. "I'm an elephant's child. I belong here with Oona,
with the orang-utans, with you. I'm staying. I'll be your
eyes and ears in the jungle."

I turned to Grandpa and Grandma then. I could see
at once in their faces that both of them understood what
I had in mind, what I was going to do.

"I'm sorry, Grandpa, sorry, Grandma. But this is my
home now," I told them. Grandma reached out to me,
pleading with me. But Grandpa put his arms round her
and held her.

"You stay, Will," he said, his eyes filled with sadness.
"If it's where you want to be, then stay. Be happy.
Grandma and me, we'll be happy, if we know you are."

I turned away and ran from them then, back down the jetty. Oona was waiting for me, where I had left her outside Geraldine's house. She saw me coming, and was kneeling for me already. I was up and on to her neck in a trice, and she was striding out across the lawn, and then we were into the jungle, Other One swinging through the trees above us, and we were running now, running wild.

Written by Will's grandfather
January 1st, 2009

I wish with my whole being that this story had never happened at all. But it did happen. And as it turned out, while it is a story that began with a tragedy, it has been in so many ways the most joyous, certainly the most important happening of my entire life, and that's in over sixty-five years. We lost a dear son, then a wonderful daughter-in-law, and we very nearly lost Will too, our grandson. But miraculously he survived, and we found one another again. Out of sorrow can come sweetness.

Then almost as soon as we'd found him again, it seemed we might be losing him, this time for ever. Once he'd disappeared into the jungle with Oona that day, his grandmother and I could not bring ourselves to leave. We made a decision, as it turned out, the best decision of our lives, we think. The long and the short of it is that we went off home to England, back to Devon, for a couple of months to sell up the farm. Then we came back here to make our lives with Geraldine and her orphan orang-utans. We wanted to be as near as we could to Will.

Geraldine always said she was sure he'd be back, and she was right. Come back he did, and he does, bringing in orphaned orang-utans from the jungle so that they can be cared for here at the orphanage. His grandmother became a minder – she's fostered three of them now, trained them up to go out into the jungle again, to be wild again. She's on her fourth. She loves it, and she does a fine job of it too – she was always good with orphan lambs back on the farm. And as for me, I bury myself in all the administration and fundraising for the orphanage, working alongside Geraldine. This is home for us now.

Will comes back as and when he needs to. He's over

[illegible] more. Each time he comes, he

It wasn't Will's idea that his story should be told, it was Geraldine's. We were all there sitting around one evening, chatting after supper and Scrabble, Will leaning up against Grandma's knee, Oona's eye looking in at the window as usual. "I've been thinking, Will," Geraldine began. "I think your story should be told; written down, I mean. It should be put in a book so people can read it. It's an important story, Will, a story everyone in the world should know, because it's full of hope and determination. And we need that. Someone should write it. It would be a very different kind of a book, because the end is still being decided, and that's because it's a living story that's still going on. The book could be part of its own story, so to speak, it could change how things turn out, how the story ends."

"I think you should write it, Grandpa," Will said. "You used to do a bit of writing, didn't you?"

"Only a little weekly column for the local paper," I told him. "I can't write a book."

"Course you can," Grandma said, "you're a good writer, and what's more you're the only one who can do it. I can't write for toffee, and Will's always coming and going on that elephant, so he can't do it, can he? You know Will better than anyone, excepting that elephant perhaps. You know both the worlds he's lived in, all the important people in his life. Go on, Grandpa, you can do it. Keep you out of mischief."

I was warming to the idea all the time they were speaking, but still unsure of myself. "What d'you really think, Will?" I asked him. "It's your story."

"Go for it," Will said, smiling up at me. "There's no one else I'd want to do it. I'll tell you everything you need to know, Grandpa, everything. Geraldine's right, people have to know what's going on out there in the jungle, before it's too late. You tell them, Grandpa. But when you write it, I want you to be me, to tell my story as I lived it, as if you were me. Can you do that?"

"I can try," I said.

Will looked up at Oona at the window.

never find the way of making such a story my own, never felt that it could be anything other than a dim echo of Kipling's two great stories. The truth is, I suppose, that I never felt *compelled* to write it.

Then a series of tragic historical happenings conspired to persuade me that this was a book I had to write, and that I *could* write. I discovered that at the present rate of attrition, orang-utans would not survive in the wild for more than five years, destruction of habitat being the main cause of this genocide. I discovered, too, that there is an extraordinary woman who has spent her whole life living in the rainforest, trying to save and then rehabilitate orphan orang-utans.

Then, on Boxing Day 2004, the Asian *tsunami* hit the coasts of Indonesia and Sri Lanka, killing hundreds of thousands of people. I learned that elephants and other animals seemed to sense the coming of the *tsunami* long before people did, many of them running up into the jungle, to high ground, to save themselves. And I heard the true story of an English boy, on holiday with his family, who was on an elephant ride along the beach when the *tsunami* came in, and whose life was saved when the elephant he was riding took fright and ran off into the jungle. It was a story of survival against all

the horror of a disaster that

the Iraq war is still fiercely debated, with some studies estimating the dead at more than half a million, and others denying such a shocking statistic. But whatever figure is right, it seems certain that at least 100,000 ordinary Iraqis – not soldiers – were killed between 2003 and 2006. We know much more accurately how many soldiers have died: to date, about 3,000 Americans and 200 British, with many thousands more injured and maimed.

Somehow these dreadful events, as well as those favourite stories of my childhood, fused together to inspire *Running Wild*. Now there seemed a real reason to write it, a *need* even.

Maybe, though, none of these was the true seed-corn of this story. Maybe it was a poster on the wall of my classroom when I was ten, a poster of the poem 'The

Tyger', written and illustrated by William Blake. I used to look at it a lot when lessons became boring, which they often did. I think it was the only poem I knew by heart when I was young, and one of the most powerful I've ever read.

Michael Morpurgo, May 2009

Many of you may want to know more about these real events, about the whole background to the making of *Running Wild*. So, in brief:

The Iraq War

Iraq is an Arab republic in South West Asia and is bordered to the north by Turkey, to the west by Syria and Jordan, to the south by Saudi Arabia, Kuwait and the Persian Gulf, and to the east by Iran. Iraq is a fairly young country, only created in 1921 by the British Government. Iraq used to be part of a much larger region, ruled by the Turks, called The Ottoman Empire. When the Ottoman Empire fell, British rule took over – until Iraq was given independence in 1932. A number of different governments controlled the country after that, until Saddam Hussein seized power in 1979. The UK and USA supported him because he was helping them to fight a neighbouring country, Iran. But it was quickly apparent that Saddam Hussein was a ruthless tyrant. He used terror to suppress all opposition. However, when Iraq invaded Kuwait for its oil in 1991, many countries – including the US and UK – joined together to force Saddam Hussein's army out of Kuwait, in what has come to be called the Gulf War.

Following the Gulf War, a decade passed. But then, around 2002, the US began to focus again on Saddam Hussein. There were fears that he might use weapons of mass destruction (WMDs) to attack Western countries – missiles that might, it was thought, have warheads containing poisonous gas or even nuclear explosives. Saddam Hussein had already used gas against the Kurds in Iraq. The US and the UK called for an invasion of Iraq, in order to destroy these weapons and prevent their use. The Iraq War began on March 20th, 2003 with the invasion of Iraq by a multinational force led by and composed almost entirely of troops from the US and the

December 30ᵗʰ 2006 in Baghdad, the Iraqi capital. But no WMDs were ever found. At the time of writing the British Army is withdrawing after six years in Iraq. The American and British governments hope that when the Iraqi army is able to take over responsibility for making the country safe, then the coalition forces can leave the country.

Iraqis voted for a new government in 2005. But some people in Iraq want all foreigners, particularly the soldiers, to leave straight away, and believe that by attacking them they will force them out. The conflict is still by no means over.

Deforestation

Indonesia is home to many famous endangered animals such as orang-utans, elephants and rhinos. Among relatively unknown endangered animals also living here are the clouded leopard, the sun bear and endemic Bornean gibbons. Borneo is the third largest island in the world and was once (around 1950) covered extensively with tropical rainforests, but the ever-increasing rate of deforestation over the last fifty years has rapidly shrunk the area of ancient Borneo's forests. Forests are home to many different animal and plant species, but are being burned, logged and cleared, in order to make way for agricultural land. The main reason for such excessive deforestation is the palm oil

337

plantations that have now replaced many ancient forest areas. Half the annual global tropical timber acquisition comes from this area. Huge forest fires in 1997 and 1998 were also responsible for significant loss of rainforest.

If the current rate of deforestation continues, many species will perish, some even before we have had the chance to study them. Forests are not only important because of the different species that use them as their habitats, but also because their trees absorb carbon dioxide, which is vital in the fight against global warming. Sadly, experts do not think that the current rate of deforestation will decrease, as the world population is constantly growing, and this will lead to even higher demands for agricultural land. Worldwide demand for palm oil is growing annually. Palm oil is found in hundreds of food and domestic products and has the potential to replace fossil fuels – for heating homes and fuelling cars, among other things.

Orang-utans

Native to Indonesia and Malaysia, Orang-utans are currently only found in the rainforests on the islands of Borneo and Sumatra. A species of great ape known for their intelligence, they live largely in trees and are the largest living arboreal animal. They have longer arms than other great apes and their hair is reddish brown. They are 'great apes' as opposed to 'monkeys' (monkeys have generally got tails) and are closely related to humans, sharing some 97% of our DNA. The word orang-utan is derived from Malay and Indonesian words 'orang', meaning person, and 'hutan', meaning forest, thus 'person of the forest'.

They are more solitary than other apes, with males

and females generally only coming together to mate. Mothers stay with their babies until the offspring reach the age of six or seven. Although orang-utans are generally passive, aggression towards other orang-utans is very common, and they can be fiercely territorial. Unlike gorillas and chimpanzees, orang-utans are not true knuckle walkers and walk on the ground by shuffling on their palms with their fingers curved inwards.

The Sumatran species is critically endangered, with only 7,300 individuals left in the wild, while the Bornean orangutan is endangered, with an estimated population of 45,000–69,000 in the wild. The destruction of their habitat by logging, mining and forest fires, as well as fragmentation by roads, has increased rapidly during the last decade. Orang-utans are hunted for their meat and for the pet trade.

It is estimated that at the present rate of attrition it is unlikely there will be any orang-utans living in the wild by 2015.

A *tsunami* is a series of waves that is created when a large volume of a body of water, such as an ocean, is rapidly displaced. It is a Japanese word, and can be literally translated as 'harbour wave'. Earthquakes, volcanic eruptions and other underwater explosions – such as detonations of nuclear devices at sea, landslides and other mass movements above or below water – all have the potential to generate a *tsunami*. A *tsunami* produces waves of water that move inland, giving the impression of an incredibly high tide. *Tsunamis* are sometimes referred to as 'tidal waves', but this is not technically correct as *tsunamis* have nothing to do with tides.

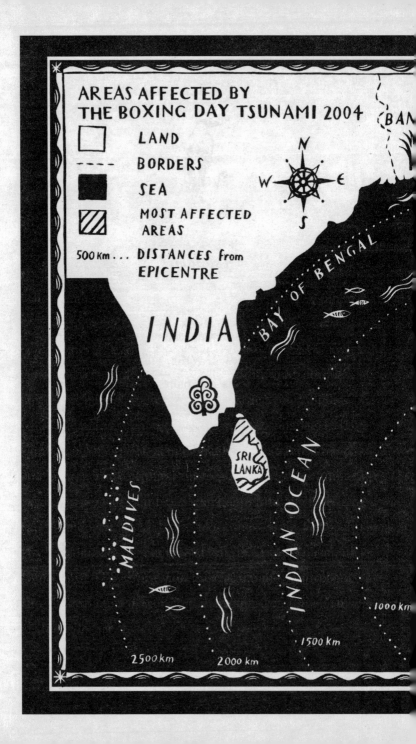

Due to the immense volumes of water and energy involved, the effects of *tsunamis* can be devastating. There is often no advance warning of an approaching *tsunami*, but some animals seem to have the ability to detect such natural phenomena.

The 2004 Indian Ocean earthquake was an undersea tremor that occurred on December 26th with its epicentre off the west coast of Sumatra in Indonesia, and the consequent *tsunami* is known as the Asian *Tsunami* or the Boxing Day *Tsunami*. Sri Lankan media sources claimed that elephants heard the sounds of the *tsunami* as it approached the coast and their reaction was to move inland, away from the approaching noise. Large numbers of children from fishing communities drowned in the *tsunami*, because when the sea was sucked away before the wave came in, they saw thousands of fish stranded on the seabed. They rushed out to catch them, only to be overwhelmed by the great wave.

Tsunamis are not rare, with at least twenty-five occurring in the last century. Many of these were recorded in the Asia-Pacific region. The Boxing Day *Tsunami* caused approximately 350,000 deaths and

And lastly, here is 'The Tyger' by William Blake, the poem that first inspired this story.

Could frame thy fearful symmetry?

In what distant deeps or skies
Burnt the fire of thine eyes?
On what wings dare he aspire?
What the hand dare seize the fire?

And what shoulder and what art
Could twist the sinews of thy heart?
And when thy heart began to beat,
What dread hand and what dread feet

What the hammer, what the chain?
In what furnace was thy brain?
What the anvil? What dread grasp
Dare its deadly terrors clasp?

When the stars threw down their spears,
And water'd heaven with their tears,
Did he smile his work to see?
Did he who made the lamb make thee?

Tyger, tyger, burning bright
In the forests of the night,
What immortal hand or eye
Dare frame thy fearful symmetry?